The Man Eating Wolves of Ashta

The Man Eating Wolves of Ashta

Ajay Singh Yadav

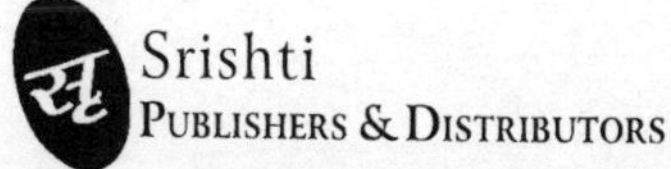

Srishti
Publishers & Distributors

SRISHTI PUBLISHERS & DISTRIBUTORS
64-A, Adhchini
Sri Aurobindo Marg
New Delhi 110 017

First published in 2000 by Srishti Publishers & Distributors

ISBN 81-87075-49-X
Rs. 125.00

Cover Design and Photography by Arrt Creations
45 Nehru Apartment, Kalkaji, New Delhi 110 019
e-mail: arrt@vsnl.com

Printed and bound in India by
Saurabh Print-O-Pack, Noida

Contents

1. LIFE AS A GUN TOTING COLLECTOR 1
2. MOUNTING PANIC 11
3. THE MAN EATER'S IMPACT ON VILLAGE LIFE 21
4. THE FIRST COUNCIL OF WAR 29
5. THE FIRST ENCOUNTER 35
6. DR HAIDER GETS HIS QUARRY 43
7. ROOP SINGH HAS HIS DAY 55
8. THE BULLOCK CART RIDE 65
9. SHAHJADE MAKES HIS APPEARANCE 75
10. A DUCK SHOOTING INTERLUDE 81

11.	THE COMMISSIONER ARRIVES	91
12.	AN UNACCOUNTABLE INCIDENT	101
13.	A REVIEW OF THE SITUATION	107
14.	A FAREWELL PARTY	115
15.	HOW THE COMPENSATION WAS SANCTIONED	125
16.	STRANGE HAPPENING IN DODI REST HOUSE	135
17.	ACHHAN MIAN'S ORCHARD	145
18.	HOW THE FIRST KILL TOOK PLACE	159
19.	HIDDEN VALLEY	163
20.	THE LAST ENCOUNTER	179

Preface

The events narrated in this book, took place in the course of a busy career in the civil service. A civil servant's life is a progression from one inconsequential matter to another, literally one damned thing after another. As a result, even if one has had the good fortune to have experienced something remarkable in the course of one's work, it is soon obliterated by the daily preoccupation with the mundane. The events relating to the man eating wolves of Ashta, therefore, lay in some corner of my mind, overlaid by a vast store of randomly acquired impressions and images, but never completely effaced by these later accretions. It was when I left the civil service, having become once more the master of my fate, that these memories came up again to the surface of the mind from the obscure depths where they had lain so long dormant, and demanded to be put down on paper. The result is this book.

This is not however a straightforward shikar yarn, on the lines of Jim Corbett's stories. Jim Corbett was not only a great shikari, he was also a master of the art of story telling. Everyone, who has tried his hand at writing a shikar story can not fail to be indebted to Corbett, just as anyone who tries his hand at drama, can not altogether ignore Shakespeare. If the reader finds many echoes of Corbett here, he can ascribe it therefore, not to any conscious imitation, but to the unconscious influence that a great figure in any field exerts on all those who come after him.

I say unconscious influence, because it is useless to imitate

Corbett deliberately. Such a thing will soon be caught out as a bogus copy of the original. Corbett is unique and beyond imitation. There may have been greater shikaris than Corbett, though I doubt if anyone has ever displayed a profounder knowledge of jungle lore, there may have been better writers than Corbett though again I doubt if many have equalled his gift for lucid, forceful expression. But it is safe to assert that there has not been, and there never will be, a great shikari who was also a great master of English prose, greater than Corbett.

The story told in the following pages is, therefore, inevitably quite a different thing, from anything written by Corbett, or indeed from most of the tales one finds in the *genre* of the Shikar yarn. This is so, first of all, because I am no shikari. My perspective is that of the administrator, who had also, in the performance of his duty, to deal with a man eating animal. Had I been a shikari, the whole story would have had quite a different resonance, I suspect. On the other hand, I have tried to add one or two vignettes of district life, to give the reader an idea of the colour and texture of the life of a district officer. Whether they have *come off*, or otherwise, I leave the reader to judge.

'This book may therefore have some documentary value and it is just as well therefore, at this stage, to answer a question which will, I fear, be asked by many who read it. This is the question of the truth of the events herein reported. Let me say for the record, that this is by and large a truthful chronicle, although some of the characters appear under assumed names while a few are purely fictitious. Again there are some things that have highlighted and retouched for dramatic effect, but on the whole, whatever is herein described, occured as reported. Only the chapter titled, 'How the compensation was sanctioned,' may be taken as a parable rather than a literal transcription of an actual incident. All the characters described in this chapter are fictitious, but the relevant point made there is – this is how things do actually happen in government. Therefore my answer to the question posed above would be the same as Mark Twain's – "there were some things in it that he stretched, but in the main he told the truth."

Life as a gun toting Collector

The story that I am going to narrate took place in the last quarter of the year 1985 and the first few months of 1986. Although more than fourteen years have passed since then, the events described herein are still fresh in my mind. Still although most of these events are vivid in my memory, it is quite possible that I may have overlooked or passed over many other material details which I should have mentioned. These lapses may be ascribed to the fact that I have not had access to the files relating to the case and have thus had to rely exclusively on my memory. If any inaccuracies are therefore discovered in this truthful chronicle by those few persons who have a closer acquaintance with the facts, they are due to this lack of documentary corroboration.

To begin at the beginning then, I was Collector of Sehore district in the year 1985. To those who are not acquainted with the administrative geography of Madhya Pradesh, Sehore is a small upcountry district adjacent to the state capital of Bhopal. The district takes its name from the district town of Sehore, a small *moffussil* town typical of the many such places in the interior regions of India. The social and political life of Sehore revolves around the district Collectorate, and the other district offices that are situated there. Imagine to yourselves a town of some fifty thousand souls, with undistinguished houses all jumbled up in crooked and narrow streets and you will have a picture of Sehore. The centre of the town is the bustling bazar, in the case of Sehore it is the bada bazar, with the usual congregation of small shops selling an assortment of articles. The most attractive of these dingy shops are the ones that sell spices and condiments, with piles of red chillies and yellow turmeric and the pungent smell of other spices heaped in neat conical piles. There are also a host of small eating places, restaurant would be too dignified an appellation for them and to call them, *dhabas* would not be strictly accurate, because they are devoid of the ethnic chic associated with that word, perhaps one might call them small dives, where the locals gather to exchange gossip. These establishments have a peculiar feature, which distinguishes them from other eating joints, they have a liberal supply of stringed charpoys and flat topped wooden *khatiyas* where the locals sit and talk interminably about all things under the sun, but chiefly about their consuming passion, politics. The streets are shared by sundry itinerant cows, which generally have the right of way over other pedestrians and thus are treated with a regard and consideration which is seldom shown to human beings. The town also boasts of a *Qasbah,* the old quarter, where the muslim population is concentrated. This is a perfect *cul de sac* of twisting backstreets and dark alleyways which peter out in dead ends. Many of the streets in the *Quasbah,* after passing through a squalid vista of huddled tenements, terminate in the onion dome and slim minarets of a mosque.

Through the town meanders a broad and shallow stream called the Seevan river. This is a river which must at one time have been a considerable stream, because there are pucca ghats at both the banks, along with the usual outcrops of small temples. These ghats have several steps, so that people can go on bathing and washing in the river even when the rising water level during the rains submerges the lower steps. But now sadly, the channel carries only a despairing thread of water, reminding one of Auden's lines :*the baltering torrent sunk to a soodling thread.* Fortunately there is a small annicut or weir built on the river, and the gates of this annicut are kept locked except in the rainy season, so that the channel fills up with water, and people can at least perform their ablutions as of yore.

The only buildings of consequence in this town are the government buildings, which include the government degree college, the central school, the sports hostel and the imposing post office. But the hub of the town is undoubtedly the collectorate complex housing the Collector's residence and office.

These are buildings dating from the hey day of the Raj. The Collector's residence and office is really one building, an old building which carries an inscription in one corner, that bears the legend 'constructed 1868'. This building which used to be the residence of the British Political Agent, is still redolent with the spirit of the raj. In the front is a pillared verandah, with a high ceiling supported on massive masonry columns. The rooms are cavernous, with parquet flooring and real fireplaces. These buildings stand in a sprawling compound. The house is fronted by a formal garden, which is enclosed by a small wilderness, where the giant bamboo, which is such a notable feature of this place grows in profusion. At the back of the house are fields which stretch away upto the river.. There are steps leading down to the water, and a private jetty where a small paddle boat is permanently moored for the use of the collector, should he feel like a cruise through the shallows. It was here that I stayed and worked as Collector of the district when the events which I am about to narrate took place.

Before I come to these events which form the subject matter of this book and which the reader is no doubt anxious to read, let me supply a few more incidental details which are germane to my story. Sehore is a largely agricultural district. The inhabitants of the district are sturdy cultivators who are brought into contact with the government only when some natural calamity like a hailstorm or a flood destroys their crops. Apart from attending to the infrequent disputes relating to land which arise now and then in all such places, the Collector has not very much to do. I remember describing the place as a 'good batting wicket', when I handed over charge to my successor. As it happens there was a horrendous communal riot just a fortnight later, where the rioters did not spare even the patients in their hospital beds, but that is another story. The point of this story is that with all this time on my hands I took to shooting ducks and other feathered game and what started as a sport soon developed into a passion. Every morning and usually every evening, I headed out for one of the numerous tanks which are situated around the town of Sehore. How well do I remember their names – Bhagwanpura, Jamonia, Lasuria, Lormi. The smell of decaying vegetation and wet earth as one hid behind the clump of ipoemia bushes to stalk the birds is still fresh in my nostrils and I can still hear the whirr and the splash of hundreds of surprised birds rising suddenly after running on the water for while ;and the resonant tonk of the bar headed goose, which I never succeeded in surprising. Although in those bloodthirsty days I did not spare any thought for the morality of what I was doing, looking back on it after all these years I feel that I was wrong to take up killing animals simply for pleasure. A few years after this I suffered a complete revulsion from all forms of killing, I gave up Shikar and turned a vegetarian, but this is to anticipate things. In those bad old days, I had no such scruples and fish, flesh and fowl, all was grist to the mill. What I did was however not illegal, because I was careful to obtain a licence from the DFO, to shoot a given number of migratory ducks. (In those days this could still be done – now of course one is forbidden to shoot even *vermin*). These daily shikar expeditions taught me the value of shooting straight and sitting still, but what is more important they brought me into touch with some of the characters who form the leading *dramatis personae* of this story and it is time to introduce them to the reader.

The first of these was Siddique, a judge who later rose to eminence in his profession. What brought him into touch with me was however our shared passion for shikar. Siddique was not a mere *chidimar* like me, he had accounted for bigger game in his time, but being a stickler for legal correctitude had now opted to follow my lead and stick to feathered game. Tall and imposing, with an aquiline profile, Siddique was also a chain smoker. Later with his elevation to the bench, he took to puffing on a pipe under the impression that this was more becoming to his exalted station in life. I shall have more to say about Siddique, but for now let me spare the personal details lest I incur the charge of contempt of court.

Dr Haidar, was a friend of Siddique and was something of a local character. Dr Haidar, was not really a doctor, he was a journalist, that is to say he was a gentleman farmer who also dabbled in journalism. He was tall, cherubic, balding and addicted to *paan* as well as cigarettes. He drove a rickety old car, a Maurice 7 of 1931 vintage which still seemed to be able negotiate the toughest terrain. Dr Haidar was distinguished for the extreme amiability of his character, for the clearness of his heart – a real gentleman if ever there was one. He was however no Shikari, he moved about with a Spanish shotgun, which he claimed had almost miraculous accuracy and firepower but I doubt if he shot so much as a rabbit with it. Nonetheless he was always game for a shikar expedition, no matter what the time, and also had a fund of shikar yarns, and was thus a good companion to have on these jaunts.

Next in the list is Ram Singh my home guard jawan, who was actually a native of Ashta Tehsil. Ram Singh was a stalwart figure, a tall upstanding man with a handlebar moustache. What made him an invaluable member of my party was however not his imposing stature but another accomplishment, he was an excellent mime, who could render to perfection the crying of a child as well as the calls of many other animals. As will be narrated later, this unusual skill was to prove the doom of one of the killer wolves. Ram Singh brought another feature to his job that was priceless-enthusiasm. Let me narrate one incident which brings out this quality of his character.

One winter evening I was sitting up for ducks on the banks of the Lasuriya tank. I had taken up my position in the lee of some bushes. Sitting on the wet damp green sward was proving to be slightly uncomfortable. To add to the discomfort a chill breeze had started blowing briskly. The sun had set and the shades of night were falling fast when I heard a flight of Pintails approaching. The birds were flying low in the typical 'V' formation, reconnoitring the tank bed before intending to settle for the night. As they came overhead I fired once, twice, thrice, and every time the sharp report of the shot gun was followed by the splash of a bird falling into the water. The funny thing about Shikar is its unpredictability. I had spent many months patiently stalking these wily birds, I had spent many uneasy hours crouching in makeshift 'hides', had spent a small fortune on paper and rubber decoys, had tried the expedient of taking a row boat to the middle of the water to wait for the ducks, but all to no avail. Yet now in the uncertain light of dusk three chance shots, fired without careful aim had all gone home and brought down three birds. But the birds had come down some distance from the shore, in fact quite a long distance from the shore, and there was this expanse of chilly water and muddy shoreline to traverse before they could be retrieved. The problem was how to accomplish this difficult task. But even before I could work out a solution Ram Singh was in the water, undaunted by the wet and the cold and wading out in the neck deep water, soon had the birds in hand. When he got back with the three fat birds dripping in his hands, he looked as happy as though he had brought them down himself. This was Ram Singh, an invaluable man to have on any Shikar party.

The other characters in this story shall be introduced as we go along the way. For the time being this cast of characters must suffice. It remains to supply the reader with some details about events immediately preceding this story. Those were the early days of Rajiv Gandhi's government. In those heady days training was a buzz word and it was assumed that there was nothing like an intensive course of training to modernise the administration. Conventional wisdom used to hold that a Collector should never leave his district for long. This old shibboleth was however set aside in favour of the new found ardour for training, and more than twenty Collectors were packed off on a four week long course of training at the state academy of administration at Bhopal. I was also one of these fortunate trainees and unlike others, who were still running their districts by remote control, I was enjoying this enforced leave of absence from the drudgery of routine when things started happening in Sehore district. The first sign of trouble came in the form of newspaper reports about the killing of a small child in Ashta tehsil by some strange animal. No one could clearly describe the animal. Some reports said it was a leopard, others described it as a hyena of monstrous size. There was no speculation at this stage about the involvement of a wolf. The first incident was quickly followed by a second and then a third killing and by now alarm bells began to ring throughout the district. The press gave headline coverage to the mysterious killing of children by some strange animal. The state government woke up to the fact that they had to contend with more than an isolated local incident, and I was ordered back to Sehore to take charge of proceedings and to deal with this snowballing menace.

Mounting Panic

When I got back to Sehore and visited Ashta the next day, I found the affected villages in the grip of rapidly spreading panic. As soon as darkness fell an unwritten curfew came into force over the entire area and no one was seen out of doors. When movement was unavoidable, people moved about in small parties armed with *laathis.* Where firearms were available these were brought out of moth balls and old muzzle loaders, matchlocks and shot guns of a vintage seldom seen, began to displayed with much pride in the bazaars and streets of the many small villages which line the Bhopal-Indore highway which went through the man eater's territory. All this however had not the slightest effect on the depredations of the man eater or man eaters as the case proved to be later. The killings continued unabated. All the precautions which people took were useless. This was because the killings always took place in daylight and people can not be made to stay indoors during the day for any length of time.

Before proceeding further it is necessary to give the reader a clear picture of the terrain where the man eater was operating. Exactly half way between Bhopal and Indore is the roadside village of Dodi, situated on the banks of the Dudhi river. If this village were taken as the centre of a circle of a radius of about 15km it would fairly enclose the territory where the man eater was active. The most remarkable feature of this area is the undulating plateau which starts at the village of Pagaria chor a few miles south west of Ashta and continues for about 10kms, ending in the village of Dodi. As one stands at the summit of the ghat before descending to Dodi one can see a vast panorama of rolling hills to the south and north and wide valley in between, through which flows the broad rocky stream called the Dudhi river. The road ascends gently to the west and fades into the forests of Dewas district on the western horizon. The valley of the Dudhi river sports patches of good cultivated land which are interspersed with innumerable rocky uplands of the kind described above. These plateaux and hillocks are well wooded on their sides, though bare on the top, and afford plenty of cover for any wild animal which needs it. Nestling in the valley in the lee of these hills are many small villages whose names the reader would do well to remember. If we take the Indore road, following an east west axis and roughly bisecting the area as our benchmark, then the main villages to the south of the road are Amala Mazzu, Gwala, Gwali, Amarpura, Rupahera and Rupeta. To the north are the villages of Dodi, Arnia Gazi, Foodra and Semli Zadid. There are of course many smaller villages whose names can be read on any survey map but are here omitted, but one village which I must mention is the small settlement of Pardhikhera, inhabited by the Pardhis, an aboriginal tribe who make their living by trapping animals. The chief of their clan, Rajaram Pardhi has to role to play in this story.

As one stands at the top of the Dodi Ghat looking west, this whole area can be seen below as one vast amphitheatre, where the green patches of cultivation interspersed with the darker green of wooded hills look like a patchwork quilt of green. Some of these hills rise abruptly from the flat country, like icebergs becalmed on a tranquil ocean. Many of these hills have flat tops, some are almost half a mile wide and in length stretch for several miles. These gently undulating hill tops with clumps of teak and miscellaneous forest provide ideal hiding places for wild animals, and one can still find hyenas, foxes and other small game, and maybe even the odd wolf in these hills. It is a rugged and beautiful terrain where looking for a man eating wolf or wolves is like looking for the proverbial needle in the haystack. But this was the area where we had to match wits with the man eater of Ashta.

To add to our problems, the predominant crop in the area during those days was jowar, a crop which grows as tall as a man. The other major crop was sugarcane, which not only grows tall but is also well nigh impenetrable. These fields of jowar and sugarcane thus provided ideal cover in which any animal could lie in wait, close to where human beings lived and worked and after securing a kill should the opportunity arise, quickly make a get away.

One other feature of the area should be mentioned, which should have worked in our favour but as things turned out did not prove to be of much use. This was the general absence of perennial streams and sources of water in the area. The Dudhi river was a purely seasonal torrent. In the rains it was a broad bosomed river but in the months of winter the black basalt of the river bed was bare of any water. Only at certain places, known only to a few locals, there were perennial pools of water in the river bed and these acted as waterholes for the animal population of the area. Considering the general lack of water in the area it would have been reasonable to assume that the man eater would also sooner or later make an appearance at one of these waterholes. Proceeding on this assumption we laid careful traps at these places. Local shikaries sat up over selected baits. Young goats were chosen as bait on the assumption that wolves have a preference for them. But for some unaccountable reason the man eater did not put in an appearance at any of these places and all our precautions proved to be of no avail.

I must also say a few words about the town of Ashta. This is a small roadside town situated about 80kms from Bhopal on the Indore Bhopal highway. The only remarkable thing about the town is the small fort which stands by the side of the road overlooking the Parvati river. The walls enclosing the fort have crumbled away, so that all that is now left is a steep sided knoll whose flat top is thickly crowded with a cluster of common looking dwelling units. The Ashta tehsil building forms an imposing edifice among these squlid mud and adobe hovels. This building houses the Ashta tehsil which gives the town its status as a tehsil town and constitutes the main reason for its existence. For the town of Ashta has grown up entirely around the nucleus of administrative offices which are situated there. Further down the road after crossing the river one comes across a picturesque building adorned with a fairy tale steeple surmounted with a real weather vane. This is the Ashta Rest House – a favourite watering hole for ministers and other VIPs on their way to Indore from Bhopal. It was here that I set up my temporary headquarters, in pursuit of the man eater.

Having thus given the reader a picture of the terrain where the whole story takes place let me take up the thread of our narrative at the point where I had left off. As I have mentioned when I returned I found the whole Tehsil and more particularly the villages situated in the area described above in a state of mounting panic. The first thing was to allay their panic by talking to the villagers and by providing armed guards at each village. This was unlikely to have any impact on the activities of the man eater but it would still provide the administration with valuable information and would reassure the villagers that the government was keenly alive to their plight and the danger that they were facing. This we immediately proceeded to do. Our first questions were naturally about the kind of animal which was involved and the manner in which the kills had taken place. From the information that we gathered, we were able to reconstruct how the second and third kills took place. At this stage no one knew where or how the first kill had taken place and the second kill was presumed to be the first. It was only later that I was able to reconstruct the circumstances of the first kill and these I shall narrate presently.

The second kill took place in village Foodra. It was the third week of November. This village is situated to the north of the Indore road in the lee of the plateau. The hillside here is clothed with a forest of teak. Below the plateau are cultivated fields, in places almost enclosed by the forest. One such field belonged to Ramlal a small farmer of the village. Ramlal's family included a wife and an only son. As the field of Jowar was now in flower and wild animals and birds did their best to damage the crop it was Ramlal's practice to spend the day guarding his crop. On the fateful day this is what he was doing. As the sun began to climb higher in the heavens, his wife and son, a child of about eight appeared, bringing his lunch with them. As the sun was now overhead, Ramlal and his wife sought the shade of a tree to eat their frugal repast. Their son, not being hungry, went off to play at the edge of the forest, as boys will. Picture to yourself the tranquil and pastoral scene, the woods surrounding the green fields, the two parents sharing their meal under the trees and the child playing, within earshot. But tragedy when it strikes, comes unexpectedly. So it was here. The tranquillity of the scene was suddenly shattered by a strangled cry and looking up from their meal, they saw their son being carried off into the forest by an animal. What manner of animal it was they could not say. It was not a tiger or a leopard, but it could have been a hyena, or a wolf, although they had never seen a wolf. It took them a while to collect their wits, but seeing their only child being thus attacked gave them courage and they ran after the animal, brandishing the lathi which Ramlal carried with him. This animal, when it saw its pursuers approaching, ran off into the forest, leaving its victim on the ground. But Ramlal was too late. His son was already dead, his stomach had been torn open and the entrails were hanging out. Disturbed at his approach, the killer had not been able to commence his meal, but this was cold comfort to the parents. Ramlal's wife fainted when she saw the horribly mutilated body of her son, but Ramlal remained composed. As he later told me, when recounting the incident, the only emotion he felt was rage. "Sahib", he later told me "this wicked animal which killed my only son, made my wife an invalid for the rest of her life and made my life a burden to me, must be killed. You are our *mai baap*. I know you have the power of the *sarkar* with you, and I also know you have a kind heart. This evil animal must fall to your bullet and I shall help you in whatever manner I can. May God be with you."

This simple faith, proclaimed with such touching confidence

in the power of the state, made me doubly determined to spare no efforts to bag the man eater. Ramlal became a useful source of local knowledge and a channel of communication with the villagers. He was to found waiting for me at the Ashta Rest House at all hours of the day and night with his axe slung over his shoulder and insisted on accompanying me on all the journeys after the man eater, though this was not always possible. And there was no happier man in the entire tehsil when we finally succeeded in ending the reign of terror let loose by the man eaters of Ashta.

The second kill took place in village Amala Majju. This is a largish village south of the Indore road. In those days it was approached only by a very rough cart track, which, as we later learnt was a favourite haunt of the man eater. This road is now a perfectly serviceable metalled road, and one can easily accomplish in about twenty minutes, a journey which then took the better part of an hour. The village is surrounded by clumps of giant tamarind and mango trees, which grow to a stalwart height here. On the outskirts of the village, hard by a grove of mango trees was the humble dwelling of Jhitru, a landless labourer. A Balahi by caste, Jhitru earned his living by working as an agricultural labourer. To supplement their meagre income his wife also took up such work as became available. When she thus went out to earn her daily bread it was her practice to take her baby with her, as there was no one at home to attend to it. This is what she had done on the fateful day. As she commenced work, she made a makeshift hammock by tying an old sari between two stout saplings that grew at the edge of the field and put her baby in it. There was nothing unusual in this. Many women do this when they go out to work and take their babies with them. Even in towns, on construction sites, one can find these make shift hammocks hanging in the shade, while the mothers work out in the sun. Jhitru's wife had done this without a second thought many a times in the past, and she had no premonition of impending disaster when she left her child in the hammock and went out to work in the field. However when she came back to feed her baby the hammock was empty. By then fear of the man eater was not yet so pervasive and Jhitru's wife at first was at a complete loss as to what might have happened to her baby. She ran to her husband who soon summoned other villagers to make up a search party to look for his son. The search party at first found nothing. But after a while some one saw a small splash of blood on a leaf. A little further, lying by the side of the track was the child's shirt, caught up in some lantana bushes which grew abundantly there and a little further down the track, at a place where a small spring welled out from a trough, were the splayed out pug marks of some animal which no one could identify. Beyond this there was nothing. One member of the search party, Hariprasad, the local Sarpanch, had heard of the earlier kill at Foodra and stories about the strange animal which was killing children. It was he who suggested that the local forest officials at Dodi should be approached for assistance. As for Jhitru and his wife, they could only mourn the death of their child and wait for such assistance as the government might provide.

The forest officials at Dodi, brought the matter to the knowledge of the Range Officer at Ashta, who in turn informed the Divisional Forest Officer at Sehore. It was from the DFO that I first heard the story, which I later confirmed from the unfortunate Jhitru and his fellow villagers of Amala Majju. According to the forest officials – the pug marks belonged to a single male wolf of giant size. Thus was born the legend of the man eater of Ashta – of an animal of supernatural size and strength, of diabolical cunning and horrific cruelty, who always seemed to be one step ahead of those who had set out to kill it.

The Man eater's impact on Village life

It is difficult for those who have never lived in a village, to form a proper notion of what happens to small community when it is confronted with an unexpected emergency of the kind represented by man eating wolves. For this reason the reader will, I hope, forgive me if I dwell at some length on the impact of this unexpected event on the lives of the denizens of the aforementioned village of Foodra, where the first kill is recorded as having taken placed.

Foodra is a smallish village of some two hundred souls, situated a little to the north of the Indore road, in the lee of Dodi Ghati. Although not too far from a busy highway, the village is not easy of access. It is approached only by a rough cart track, which is not serviceable in the rainy season. The village is also enclosed by a small forest, which makes it more isolated than other villages in the neighbourhood. Like most other villages in the plains of India, the settlement consists of mud and adobe houses all huddled together in a central cluster or *abadi*, the living space being, surrounded by cultivation. The houses are all built together, in a dense tangle, because this gives a feeling of security to the villagers and perhaps, in the older days it did gave them some protection from bandits and pindaris. At any rate, this system of a nucleus of dwelling units, surrounded by cultivated fields has always been the basic plan of an Indian village since times immemorial, and only a few intrepid souls live in homesteads outside the main *abadi*.

The village of Foodra is built on the plan of rough E, with the main street forming the long arm of the E and the the three lateral extensions, where the less prosperous members of the community live, forming the short arms. The village stands on a slight elevation, so that it can be seen as a cluster of red and brown tiled roofs, peeping over the thick foliage of a grove of mango trees that lies just before it.

Almost the first thing that one comes across on entering the village is the village tank, formed by bunding a rain water channel. The rain water thus impounded forms a rather enticing sheet of water, one corner of which is entirely covered by the broad leaved lotus and water hyacinth. On the low irregular embankment stands a small *shivalaya*, a tiny tent like temple dedicated to shiva. The temple is shaded by the overarching branches of a gigantic Peepul tree, which has always stood like a guardian over the tutelary deity of the village.

Entering the village proper one beholds a long straggling row of houses on both sides of an unpaved street, where the earth is compacted hard due to the constantly passing hooves of the village cattle. The same cattle churn the black volcanic earth into an ankle deep cauldron of mud during the rainy season, but that is an inconvenience seldom encountered by strangers, because strangers do not come this way in the rains. This street, which is the main street of the village, forming the long arm of the E spoken of earlier, consists of mud and adobe houses, with sloping tiled roofs. The only house of consequence in this street is the house of Dan Singh Patel, the *mukkadam* of the village. This house stands in the centre of the street, and consists of a long whitewashed wall, in the middle of which is an imposing wooden gateway. This gateway opens out into a covered passage on both sides of which is a large open parlour where chairs and *morhas* (rush seats) are laid out for visitors. The passage leads onto a large courtyard beyond which are the residential quarters.

The owner of this hacienda, Dan Singh Patel, was at the time of this story a middle aged man, who always sported a three to four days old stubble on his chin. This untidy beard was accompanied by a neat toothbrush moustache, which looked rather incongruous on his sallow face. Dan Singh was reputed to have a foul temper, but was rather a good man really, as the reader will see presently.

I have mentioned that RamLal the father of the boy who was the wolf's first victim lived in village Foodra. It was to his house that I now went. My purpose was to condole with him the death of his son. The occasion was the thirteenth day ceremony of his son. Ram Lal had displayed a naïve faith in my ability to avenge the death of his son and been a more or less permanent fixture at the Rest House whenever I happened to be in Ashta, which was quite often. The least I could do under the circumstances was to show my solidarity with him and so to his house I decided to bend my steps. Ram Lal's house was a much humbler affair than the *bada* of Dan Singh Patel. It was built, like most of the other houses in the village, of mud walls, plastered with mixture of lime and yellow earth. The house was really made up of two rectangular enclosures, the smaller enclosure being situated within the larger one. The inner rectangle was the main living room, while the outer rectangle formed a closed veranda which ran round the inner room and served various assorted needs. The front portion of this veranda, was also used as a sitting room, and it was here that all the guests were to sit.

Ram Lal led me first to a small dais where a picture of his son was placed. Here I garlanded the picture and lit a few *agarbattis* before it. There was already a pile of flowers and garlands around the picture, which was almost smothered in flowers. A pandit was conducting a havan, in one corner where a small altar had been built. I was conducted to a seat close to the altar or *vedi* as it is called, and allowed to take part in the yagya as a guest of honour. The pandit a portly gentleman clad in a resplendent red dhoti and a white *angavastram* presided over the pooja with great *elan*. He seemed to know the mantras, which formed the body of the ritual by heart and intoned them with a pedantic deliberateness, annunciating the sanskrit syallbles with clarity and relish.. At the end of each mantra he would pause and then exclaim, 'swaha 'with great solemnity. At his command all of us would throw handfuls of the oblation, which consisted of unhusked paddy, camphor and other aromatic substances into the fire. The room was filled with a thick fragrant smoke and the incantation of vedic hymns. A conch shell was taken up and blown by the pandit at the end of the puja.

After this pooja we were led to another portion of the veranda where all of us were seated on the ground in two long rows facing each other, to partake of the ritual feast. Ram Lal had placed me in the centre of the row with Dan Singh Patel next to me, and the other village notables around us.. Now that the pooja was over and ceremonial tributes had been paid to the memory of the departed soul, tongues were loosened and everyone was anxious to tell me his own personal grievance against the wolf. One skinny, little man, who was waiting for an opportunity to speak, now rose up to deliver an oration, but was asked to continue sitting and to narrate his woes, without taking the trouble to stand. This is what he had to say –

"Sahib, we thank you for having visited our far off village. Indeed if memory serves me right, you are the first Collector to have set foot in this village. We are grateful to you for this favour, but sir!,your coming here will be fruitful only if this wolf, this *shaitan*, is soon destroyed. Otherwise Sahib, we are heading for ruin. As all my brothers here will tell you, the outlying fields have gone out of cultivation for fear of the man eater as most people are afraid to go so far afield. No one stirs out of his house after daylight, even if some one is ill, that person must continue to suffer and hang on until it is daylight. And we have given up going into the forest for our daily needs. If some one needs a few pieces of timber to repair his house he must go to the forest depot and pay thorough his nose for a few rickety poles, which he could formerly get for nothing from the forest. Worst of all, many parents have stopped sending their children to school, for fear that may be attacked on the way. If things go on like this, our children will grow up to be illiterates like us, and what can be worse than that. "

There was a murmur of assent at this and a tall strapping lad, who seemed to be a college going youth and therefore well qualified to speak on the subject of education said, "Shambhu, is absolutely right sir! but he has forgotten to add one thing, ever since the wolf came on the scene, sanitary conditions in the village are much worse as people are afraid to stir out of doors at night. I am afraid there may be outbreak of some disease if things do not improve."

This again povoked a general agreement. Now Dan Singh Patel cleared his throat to speak." Sahib, you are our *maibaap,* our protector, and it is natural for us to thus unburden ourselves before you, for where else can we go. This is a small village, without proper roads, or streets or even a school, but sir! this lack of amenities, we are used to. We know that the government will in due course of time remedy this, but this new problem that has afflicted the village is something that has completely confounded us. In all my life, I do not know of any thing of this nature. We have lived for a long time in the midst of wild animals. There used to be a time, not so long ago, when there were tigers to be seen in the jungles of Rampur, and even now there may be some in the nearby jungles of Dewas, but who has ever heard of an animal that preys on man. This is against the laws of nature. We request you, to do all you can to save us from this terrible scourge, otherwise Sahib, as Shambhu said, we are indeed ruined."

I listened to this little speech with complete sympathy. I knew what the villagers were passing through and I assured them that the government would do all in its power to safeguard their lives. I assured them that it was only a matter of time before the man eater was eliminated. I sounded much more confident than I felt as I took my leave of the villagers.

But in one respect the wolf's visitation proved to be a blessing in disguise for the villagers of Foodra. It brought them together and destroyed the fine distinctions of caste and status that divided them. A community under siege can not afford to practice the discriminations ordained by convention. So when Jhagru's wife was suddenly sticken with severe labour pains one night and there was no one to attend to her in the village,

Dan Singh Patel himself, escorted the sick person and her attendants with his rifle, to the Primary Health Centre at Ashta and caste distinctions were forgotten. The child, when born, was named Dan Singh by the grateful parents in honour of his unexpected benefactor and today must be young lad himself.

The first Council of War

After gathering all the information that we could about the first two kills we decided to meet in the Dodi Rest House to prepare our strategy for tackling the man eater. I have already described the topography of the village of Dodi, situated on the banks of the Dudhi river, this is a roadside hamlet, typical of the many such villages to be found by the side of the Indore-Bhopal highway. Its location – roughly half way between Indore and Bhopal makes it a favourite stop over for those travelling between these two cities. The chief building of this place is the PWD Rest House, a solid masonry structure, with two identical rooms situated beside a central hall. This ordinary looking building stands right at the side of the highway in a large compound of its own. There is nothing remarkable about the building, but as the reader shall see later, unusual things do happen there sometimes.

As this building was situated in the heart of the man eater's territory it suggested itself as the natural place to convene the first council of war – so to speak. A few words should be said about the people who gathered at this conclave. The first of these was Bruno D'cruz, the district Superintendent of police. D'cruz, whose untimely death was universally mourned, was a man loved by all those who knew him. He was a hard drinking, hard driving, hard working man who did nothing by halves. D'cruz was proud of his marksmanship, as he was of his physical strength. Once, to prove a point he raised the solid iron axle of a railway carriage overhead, in one smooth hoist. He could also do one arm press ups. He was certainly fond of his drink, but then so are a number of lesser beings who have risen to the top. D'cruz was warm hearted and generous to a fault, and no one was sadder than I when his career ran into trouble over the usual trifling matters. An adverse remark, made almost in passing, by a censorious superior, was enough to destroy the career and ultimately to take the life of this lovable human being. But all this was still in the future, in those far off days, D'cruz was still in the prime of life, fit and strong and game for everything.

The Divisional Forest Officer in those days was Chaudhry, a young officer in his first divisional charge, ideally he should have been one of the heroes of the story, but somehow, he doesn't seem to figure very largely in this narrative, instead it is his two Assitant Conservators, Shrivastava and then Naqvi, who played the stellar role on behalf of the forest department. Shrivastava, quiet and efficient, did commendable work in organizing the whole operation in the initial stages. Naqvi, who shall be mentioned in the dispatches at a later stage, was more of a character, brash, excitable, and prone to bouts of violent enthusiasm, he made a lively member of the party.

I must also mention the long suffering Kaurav, the Sub Divisional Officer of Ashta, who had never ventured on a Shikar in his life, but tried manfully to rise to the challenge. I remember one morning in particular, when news was brought to us that a wolf had been sighted in village Semli Jadid, on the extreme South West on the Dewas border. I was on the spot within an hour, with a party of SAF Jawans armed with 303 rifles and Kaurav unarmed but willing to play his bit. I asked one of the Jawans to give him a rifle. We soon fanned out in a large semicircle and started combing the fields and the rough country that led into the forest and the neighbouring hills. As the sun rose higher, the going got tougher, but there was no sign of the wolf. After walking thus, with our eyes peeled, our hands on the trigger, our nerves tingling, I realized the futility of looking for the wolf in the vast stretch of broken country that we were walking through. We therefore gave up the chase and returned to our vehicles, but this unaccustomed exertion proved too much for Kaurav, who fell ill that very day, and was bed ridden for the better part of a week. Notwithstanding this misadventure, Kaurav looked after the logistical side of the operation, the provision of guns and cartridges as well as Shikaris and not least the task of providing food at irregular hours, to all and sundry. His successor Sharma was a tall personable man with a ready smile and a bluff and genial manner who also played a notable part in this story at a later stage.

That day those of us who sat down around the old dining table at Dodi Rest House included D'cruz, Shrivastava, Kaurav, and myself. D'cruz had a simple idea, saturate the whole area with an army of armed policeman and sooner or later they will shoot down the man eater. I explained to him that killing a man eating wolf was a different kettle of fish from killing a dacoit in the ravines of Chambal, and in any case I could not risk the consequences of surrendering the area to the fancies of a whole posse of trigger happy cops. For one thing they might come in each others way, and shoot each other rather than the elusive animal. For another thing they might scare away the animal, even if it were to fall into any trap that we might lay for it. "No," I told him politely but firmly, "the remedy proposed was worse than the disease and some other option would have to be considered."

Shrivastava suggested tying up baits at selected spots and putting up local shikaris and forest department sharpshooters over these baits. This idea seemed to make more sense and we agreed with his suggestions. Shrivastava also felt that we should rope in the wild life experts at Bhopal, chief of whom was Mr Lad, the chief wild life warden. This too was agreed upon.

After much deliberation and disputation – this was what we decided –

1. Baits should be tied up at Rupahera. Amal Mazzu, Gwala, Arnia Gazi and the Dodi Plateau. These baits, consisting of young goats or sheep,should be tied up, either at water holes or game trails frequented by the man eater. Shikaris, armed with. 12 bore shot guns should sit over these baits.
2. Shikaris should also sit in ambush, concealed in carefully constructed hides, situated by the side of game trails or other spots which we had reason to suspect were used by the man eater.
3. Police pickets should be posted at all the affected villages to keep up morale and to assist search parties should the need arise.
4. There should be four mobile patrolling parties, moving over the area at all times of the day and night.

These elaborate arrangements – dictated both by common sense and logic should have definitely brought the man eater's activities to a stop, but as luck would have it they had not the slightest effect on the killings, which continued unabated.

The first encounter

Just as we were concluding our meeting, Dr Haidar arrived in his Austen 7 and more to humour him than for any other reason, I decided to ride back to Ashta with him and sent the other vehicles back in advance. Dr Haidar was accompanied by Siddique his inseparable companion on these jaunts. After having a cup of tea with these two amateur Shikaris, we set off on our return journey. Just after ascending the ghat from the Dodi side, one comes to a spot, a little to the right of the road, where there used to be a large pool of water. This pool normally had abundant water till the onset of summer and was often used as a waterhole by cattle as well other animals. As we reached this spot, on a sudden hunch I asked Dr Haidar to drive on to this pool. Alighting close to the pool and making a careful circuit on foot I was able to see the faint but distinct foot prints of a large wolf on the margin of the water. I was looking at these pug marks when our attention was drawn to a man, far below us in the valley, who was running towards us and gesticulating wildly. It was not difficult to guess that the information he had to impart to us must be something to do with the wolf. Accordingly we jumped into the old car and set off – back on the road we had just traversed.

We caught up with the flustered man a little in advance of the village of Dodi. It took him a while to catch his breath and this was the story he had to tell – "Sahib, I was told that you were at the Rest House and I had run up there when I was told that you had just left. Just as I was wondering what to do, some one pointed out that you and Dr sahib were standing at the water hole on the track that goes to Rupahera, and seeing you I was running as hard as I could to catch up with you. Sahib, you must come quickly if you want to catch the man eater. It is a most enormous animal and will surely disappear into the forest if we delay any longer. Sahib! I was grazing my herd on the plateau at Arnia Gazi, when I saw or rather sensed that some strange animal was following us. I could also sense the uneasiness which the goats had started feeling. Just then this enormous brute dashed out from behind a rock and took away a beautiful kid that was not a month old. Sahib! I shouted at the animal and ran after it with my lathi, but what can a single man do beside such an animal. It soon disappeared into the jungle with my goat. Sahib if you come quickly, there is just a chance that you might be able to get a shot at it."

After a brief confabulation, we decided to rush to the spot and take our chance. It is true that our vehicle was a venerable machine which could not do more than 10knots an hour, and we had no search lights. As the sun was then close to setting we would have to take the risk of shooting at the wolf by the light of the moon. However the moon would soon be up and as it would be at the full, the light would be good enough to shoot by. I was armed with a long barrelled. 12 bore shot gun with long range double B cartridges and Dr Haidar had his fabled matchlock. Taking the distraught villager with us, we were soon climbing over the boulder strewn track that leads to the plateau of Arnia Gazi.

The track which we were following would have been difficult even for a bullock cart. It was deeply rutted and the central portion between the ruts formed a steep ridge that would have sooner or later broken the differential chamber or the axle of a lesser car. But the brave little vehicle went chugging up the gradient, bouncing up and down on the boulders like a boat bobbing on rough waters. It was here that Dr Haidar showed his dexterity with the wheel. The severe jolts, and the twists and turns in the track would have jerked the wheel clean out of the hands of less experienced pilot. But Dr Haidar knew his car, as a trained rider knows his mount, he knew just when to give it free rein and when to hold it in check. Thus by dint of alternatively gunning the engine at full throttle while riding the clutch, and at times letting the car have its head when faced with a particularly nasty boulder, so that it went over the obstruction like a bucking steed, we soon made it to the top of the plateau.

Once on the top the going was easier. Here the ground was relatively flat, and the firm red earth allowed the car to show its paces. By now the moon had risen, and the flood of silvery radiance, enabled us to see things quite clearly. The top of the plateau had a park like ambience, with clumps of large trees and lantana bushes standing here and there on the open, gently rolling country. Our guide was leading us on to a ravine on the southern edge of the plateau. Having arrived at the opening of the ravine we left the car, the rest of our journey would have to be completed on foot ;as the sides of the ravine were too steep to be negotiated by any vehicle.

As the ravine was still in deep shadow and we had no lights with us, the advisability of going down was discussed in whispers. Finally it was decided to prepare a make shift torch – this was down by winding a old shirt round and round a stick and dipping it in the petrol tank of the Austen 7. When it was set alight, this improvised torch gave out a bright light that would last us for five to seven minutes. That would be enough to make a quick reconnaissance of the ravine, and should the man eater be lurking there; to have a crack at it. So down we went into the ravine, Siddique leading the way with the torch in his hands, I behind him and Dr Haidar bringing up the rear. Our guide was too frightened to come down and elected to stay put in the car with the windows up and the doors shut and locked.

Nor did I blame him, this ravine was an eerie place, full of enormous rocks that lay all round its rather flat bottom as though some gigantic force had arranged them there. The flames of our make shift torch cast their lurid light over this strange scene and made the shadows seem even darker. Almost exactly in the centre of the rude semicircle of those druidical stones, like the sacrificial victim of some mysterious rite, lay the carcass of the goat, its belly slit open and the downy white fur spattered with blood. Obviously the wolf was somewhere close by and watching us. But it was impossible to see beyond the narrow circle of light cast by the flames. The darkness enclosed us like a curtain, and it was no use trying to peer into it to see any thing. As luck would have it the torch burned out much sooner than we had expected, leaving us in complete darkness.

There we were then, benighted at the bottom of a ravine, where, for all we knew, a man eating wolf lurked, and though there were three of us, and thus we were not in any immediate danger, we did feel that our rash descent into the ravine had turned the tables and placed us completely at the mercy of the man eater should it have any designs on us. There was however one factor in our favour. Within a few minutes, the moon would rise sufficiently high to throw its light into the ravine and then the advantage would again be with us.

So we stood stock still, holding our breaths and waiting for the moon to appear over the rim of the ravine. A dead hush descended over the scene. Even the crickets seem to fall silent. There constant shrilling provides a companionable chorus in the solitude of the jungle. There sudden silence made the stillness seem unnatural. We could sense the wolf watching us, but there was nothing we could do but wait. So we waited, looking up at the starlit sky where the moon might appear at any moment. Nor did we have long to wait. Suddenly, unexpectedly, the huge, brilliant orb of the moon appeared over the rim of the ravine. But as we looked up at the moon we saw a strange sight, silhouetted in the resplendent orb was an enormous wolf – its ears standing up stiffly, its eyes burning redly, looking straight down at us. Dr Haidar and I both raised our rifles and fired almost at the same time but both the hurriedly taken shots missed their mark and with a growl, the wolf jumped off the rocks and disappeared into the darkness.

It was now useless to wait further in the ravine because we knew that the wolf would not make a second appearance. So we clambered out and on reaching the top, paused to steady our tingling nerves. Siddique lit a cigarette. Dr Haidar claimed that he had hit the wolf and it would be soon be found dead somewhere close by. But just then the darkness and stillness of the night was rent by a thrilling sound, a low sobbing ululation that soon rose in volume and pitch to sound like the banshee wailing of a distant siren. A curiously human, eerie, but not unmelodious sound – the howling of a wolf. It was throwing us its own challenge, and perhaps mocking us at our slip shod attempts to get at it. This was the first time I had heard a wolf howling and I will not forget the moment.

Dr Haider gets his quarry

A fortnight had passed since the arrangements described above had been put in place but so far they had had not the slightest effect on the activities of the man eater. None of the baits tied at carefully selected places had been taken by the man eater. Nor had any animal been sighted at the waterholes where the Shikaris were lying in ambush. We had also put up carefully constructed hides where forest department marksmen had been put in, but so far they had seen nothing of the man eater. It was clear that we were dealing with a clever animal that was unlikely to accept baits, or fall into traps laid for it. The brief encounter that I have described above was the only sighting of the man eater to date – apart from the fleeting glimpse of the animal obtained by Ram Lal when his son was killed. This was when Dr Haidar, either by pure serendipity, or as he himself put it, by use of the sixth sense which all seasoned Shikaris possess, stumbled upon the wolf's lair. Let this part of the story be told in his own words.

"Ever since the news of the man eater of Ashta was brought to me, my mind had been in a whirl. I knew our Collector was a good man and would spare no efforts to get the man eater, but he needed all the help he could get. The men around him were nincompoops. They knew nothing about Shikar. What he needed was a man like me, a man who knew all about Shikar that there was to know, and some one who could be counted upon to shoot straight in a tight spot. The problem was, the Collector was always surrounded by busybodies and jackanapes of all kinds and I would have to make an attempt on my own, if we were to get the animal.

Thus it was that I set out one morning for Ashta, in my beloved Austen 7. I know I am often blamed for losing my head over a mere car, but I can hardly resist telling you a thing or two about this old beauty. First of all I maintain, this car can go where no other car in the district can reach. Forget about dumpy old Ambassadors and squat little Fiats, I say this car can go where even four wheel drive jeeps do not dare to venture. Why the other day, when we went after the wolf at Arnia Gazi, as the Collector will tell you, but for this brave little car, we would never have made it to the spot. Secondly this car has an elegance, a panache, an old wolld grace which is a thing not to found in modern cars. But enough, let me get on with my story.

As I was saying, it was a cold clear morning, with a stiffish breeze blowing from the north, when I set out for Ashta, and it was getting to be about eight when I reached that town. It is my practice, not to venture out on a Shikar on an empty stomach, because one never knows when the next meal would be forthcoming. I therefore decided to have a light meal at Ashta Rest House, nothing substantial, you will understand, just a few poached eggs followed by a roast chicken with a bit of biryani for the road. By the time I was through with this meagre repast, followed by a brief siesta, it was getting to be almost midnoon. There was no time to lose, so I set out immediately in the direction of Dodi.

A little short of Dodi, there is a track which turns left for the village of Amla Mazzu. If one follows this track for a few miles, and then turns off to the right on a thin strip of road that looks little more than a bridle path, one soon reaches a desolate plain, that looks like a lava plain. Nothing seems to grow in the stony, sterile earth on this stretch of the country, but there are innumerable caverns and hollows in the small hill that stands at this spot, and it was my intention to search this hill. It was my hunch that the wolf had his lair, in one of these caverns on the hill side.

To this hill then I made my way, and thanks to my car, I was there in less than an hour. I had looked into all the caverns and was about to turn away disappointed when I saw out of the corner of my eyes, something moving a little way up the hill. Sure enough this was a small cave that I had missed. A Blue Jay was sitting on a bush at the entrance of this cave. Now I admit I am superstitious and I took this Blue Jay to be an omen. I was sure that the wolf was in this cave, but I hesitated to enter this cave directly from the front, because I was afraid. Don't get me wrong. I was afraid that I might scare the wolf away, which could make a dash for the entrance of the cave and get past me in the uncertain light inside the cave. The best policy then would be to wait outside, after concealing oneself and to shoot the wolf when it came out, as I felt sure that it must.

As I was waiting outside the cave under cover of a convenient lantana bush, I saw two small balls of fur, mottled black and brown. They looked like two puppies, playful frisky and, lovable. They were the wolf cubs, and I knew by now that their mother must be somewhere nearby. I was sure she must appear on the scene any moment, and had put my shot gun to the shoulder in anticipation when I heard two shots fired in quick succession and then a small commotion, as a party of armed policemen appeared on the scene. They had sighted the wolf on their patrol, and some trigger happy members of the party had fired on the wolf without taking proper aim. They claimed to have hit the wolf but I knew better. To hit a moving target in the uncertain light of the evening without taking careful aim would have been impossible. By their rash act these novice marksmen had frittered away a golden chance of bagging the man eater and spoiled my own chances of ridding the area of this menace. I thought over the whole matter for a while. I realized that if I told them about the cave and the wolf cubs; they would barge into the cave as well and that would be the end of whatever little chance there still remained of bagging the wolf.

No I would have to keep quiet over the matter. A plan was already forming in my head. The entrance to the cave was mantled with overhanging creepers, therefore it would not have been possible to effect entry without making at least some noise thereby losing the element of surprise. A frontal assault was therefore clearly inadvisable. On the other hand the chances of lying in wait for the wolf and surprising it, as it came back to its hideout were good, but one could not rule out unforeseen disruptions of the kind that I have just described.

This was a matter therefore that called for the skills of my friend Rajaram Pardhi. Rajaram was the chief of Pardhis and the headman of the village of Pardhikhera that was not far from the spot where the lair was. The Pardhis, are past masters at the art of trapping game. They make ingenious traps and nets for snaring all kinds of birds and beasts. Classified as a scheduled tribe, most of them lead a semi nomadic existence, moving from place with their baggage piled up in caravans of bullock carts and eke out a precarious living from the more or less illegal occupation of hunting. Years ago Rajaram and I had hunted sand grouse in these parts. Rajaram had an old blunderbuss – a muzzle loader with a split barrel tied up with lashings of brass wire – of which he was inordinately proud. When fired, this gun let out a blinding flash followed by clouds of evil black smoke, which certainly blinded the user momentarily, even when they had little effect on the intended victim. More to humour Rajaram than for any other reason, I often let him handle my own double barrelled Spanish shot gun that had no equal in accuracy and range, and by dint of this generosity, I had won his permanent regard. What I proposed to do now was to summon Rajaram and his tribe to the spot and instruct them to snare the wolf in one of their clever traps. Accordingly it was to Rajaram's camp that I repaired.

Rajaram was as usual glad to see me but I had to decline his offer of hospitality on this occasion. His notions of entertainment had a touch of barbaric splendour. An honoured guest had to offered liberal doses of the fiery liquor which was brewed in house. After this there would be some dancing and singing by younger members of the tribe and all this would be followed by a meal which had to have some fresh game, if nothing else a wild boar would be roasted. The honour of the tribe required that these ceremonies be observed and observed they were, with a most scrupulous regard. However I was now getting on in years and no longer had any appetite for these dissipations. So after politely declining his proffered hospitality, I explained to him the errand that had brought me there. The first question that he asked me was, if the cubs were still there.

He felt that if the cubs were still in the cave it would be a comparatively simple matter to tap the wolf'.What he proposed to do was this. A small pit about six feet and four feet wide would be dug. This would then be covered over with twigs and earth, so that it would be completely undetectable. The wolf cubs would then be placed over this pit and tied to a small stake. The twigs and branches covering the pit would support the weight of the cubs, who were merely two small mites, but would give way under the wolf, when it came to the cubs.

To things were absolutely essential to make the trap successful. First the trap should be so well concealed that the wolf would suspect nothing. This required a great deal of skill in laying the branches over the pit and then covering it with earth. Secondly the branches must immediately give way, as soon as the wolf stepped on them. If this did not happen suddenly and immediately, the wolf would have sufficient time to jump clear and save itself. Once the animal was in the pit, it would have absolutely no chance of getting out. The Pardhis would see to that.

In accordance with the plan therefore, the next day, when the sun was well up and the cubs were likely to be alone in the cave the trap was laid. The first thing that we had to do on reaching the cave, was to make sure that the wolf was not in the vicinity. In order to do this three Pardhis, armed with stout clubs entered the cave. A score of other tribesmen, similarly armed, stood outside, ready to fall on the wolf, should it attempt to make a run for it.

I also entered the cave with the Pardhis. We went in expecting the wolf to charge us, but when our eyes got used to the dim light of the interior, we saw that the she wolf was not in the cave. The cavern was surprisingly large, considering the narrow opening. There was a strong musty odour inside. The two cubs, alarmed at the invasion of their hitherto inviolate sanctuary, were cowering in one corner. It took us only a few minutes to capture the cubs who made whimpering noises as we gathered them up in our arms walked out of the cave and into the bright light of the day.

Once the cubs were in our hands, the rest of the trap was soon set. The pit was rapidly dug and expertly camouflaged with branches and earth and two cubs were then tied to the stake and set to gambol freely on the surface. The big question now was where we should conceal ourselves. If such a large number of men remained in close proximity of the cave, the wolf would be sure to detect their presence. It was therefore decided that only Rajaram and two of his stoutest henchmen should remain on the scene along with me. However here an unexpected problem presented itself. There were no suitable hiding places close to the trap, and if we positioned ourselves too far from it there was the off chance that the wolf might make good its escape. This is where the jungle craft of the Pardhis came in handy. There were two lantana bushes growing not far from the entrance to the cave. I said to Rajaram that if only these bushes were bigger and bushier, they might offer a suitable place to hide. This was sufficient to spur him into action. After making a quick recce of the surrounding area, the Pardhis picked out three or four lantana bushes that grew a little distance from the scene. Bushes closer to the spot were rejected, because I was told that any change in their profile might alert the wolf and make it suspicious. The selected bushes were then carefully cut down almost flush with the ground, so as not to leave any tell tale stumps remaining. These bushes were then transported to the site where the hide was to be constructed and placed round the existing lantana bushes with such art that no one could tell which of the bushes were real. The bushes were so arranged that they made a small enclosure where the four of us could conceal ourselves, without any possibility of detection. There was one factor however, which could still upset our carefully laid plan and this was the direction of the wind. Although we had so positioned our hide that we would be down wind from the wolf when she arrived, any sudden change in the direction of the wind, or the expected line of approach of the wolf, would be sufficient to forewarn it of our presence. There was nothing for it however, but to conceal ourselves and sit down to await developments.

This is what we proceeded to do. The Pardhis, being children of the woods, know the art of sitting still, but for my part I find it hard to sit like a graven image, without talking, smoking or even clearing my throat, but this discipline would now have to followed, because any movement or sound from us could give away our carefully concealed position. Time passed slowly as it always does when one is waiting for something to happen. When the sun was close to the western horizon, a large black crow, perhaps I should describe it as a raven, flew over us, croaking loudly. The unexpected appearance of this bird and the way in which seemed to be behaving seemed to indicate the presence of some predator, which in this case could only be the wolf. A pebble came rolling down the hillside, bouncing over the stony surface of the black volcanic rocks and startling us badly. And a moment later the wolf appeared on the scene, a medium sized animal, much like an Alsatian dog, with a mottled greyish brown coat, she approached the cave warily, turning her head first to the left and then to the right to survey the area. But just then she spotted her cubs and her maternal instincts took over. She dashed to the spot, and fell straight into the trap laid for her. No sooner was she in the pit, then the Pardhis, with a whoop, dashed out of the hide and a rain of blows fell on the wolf. Trapped within the confines of the pit, she could not put up even the semblance of a fight, her back was broken and within a few moment she was dead. The two cubs, who were unharmed during the whole episode, were taken over by the Pardhis, in whose custody they remained for several years. What finally happened to them I do not know."

Thus ended the chronicle of Dr Haidar. When I was informed of the incident, I was in Ashta and upon reaching the village, found the wolf laid out in the middle of a circle of Pardhis, who were performing a kind of war dance over the dead animal. This wolf was not the enormous animal, that we had seen the other day in the ravine at Arnia Gazi, and we were in a sense disappointed. There was a school of thought among the forest officials who believed that we had killed the wrong animal, and they were disposed to blame Dr Haidar for this, but a post-mortem carried out on the dead animal, discovered strands of human hair and splinters of bone in its viscera. There was no doubt that we had killed a man eating wolf. It was now clear that we were dealing, not with a single man eater, but with a whole pack that had taken to human flesh. How many of these animals, were actually there, was something that could only be discovered in the course of time, but our battle against the man eating wolves of Ashta was far from over. Indeed, it had barely started. It was not a heartening thought.

Roop Singh has his day

The twin villages of Rupeta and Rupahera were one of the worst affected by the activities of the man eater. Between them they had lost four children to the wolves and the man eater's pug marks were constantly seen on the bridle paths and cart tracks leading up to these villages. Both these villages lie to the south of the Dodi ghati towards the Ashta end. Both the villages are situated in the lee of the rocky headlands that make up the south western edge of the Dodi plateau and both are fringed by a small forest of teak and other miscellaneous trees. Of the two, the village of Rupahera appeared to be more frequented by the man eater, and it is to this village that I must now take the reader for the next episode of our story.

I have mentioned the small but perennial pool of water that stands a little to the west of the Indore road at the Dodi end of the ghat. To the left of this pool a kuccha road heads out almost due south, passing over the rolling plateau. After traversing an undulating and rugged country, it reaches the plains and then bifurcates, one branch turning left to the village of Rupahera and the other branch going on to the village of Amla Mazzu, several miles to the west. The longer branch of this road is bordered by a range of low hills to the north and Jowar fields to the south. On this track, every morning were seen the pug marks of a large wolf. One morning, when we were on the spot before the crack of dawn, we saw that the pug marks were absolutely fresh, little trickles of dust, were still falling back into the sharp indentations made into the soft dust. The wolf was therefore just ahead of us, and if we were lucky might be able to surprise it. If we followed the wolf and tried to overtake it on the track, the wolf would, of a certainty get wind of us, as we were walking up wind and the wolf was ahead of us. But if we made a quick detour around one of the small hills to the right, and positioned ourselves at the spot where the path which went around the hill rejoined the track, we would get ahead of the wolf and might be able to get an easy shot at the unwary animal.

It must have been nearly a kilometre round the hill before the path rejoined the track. In places the trail all but disappeared and, at all times it was a rough and boulder strewn path that we were running on, yet we completed our circuit in double quick time to take up our position behind a pile of rocks, that stood beside the track. A quarter of an hour passed as we waited tensely. By our reckoning the wolf should have by now passed us. A half hour passed, and the sun was beginning to rise. Obviously something had gone wrong with our plan and we left our hide to investigate. After going down the track for a few hundred yards we came across the pug marks of the wolf. For some inexplicable reason, after walking in the middle of the track all along the way, the wolf had turned sharply to the left and gone of into the fields of Jowar to the south of the track. It was impossible to say why the animal had behaved in this fashion. Perhaps, it possessed a sixth sense which warned it of impending danger, and it was this sixth sense that had made it leave the track, just a few hundred yards short of the place where we were waiting in ambush. We shall never know. I mention this little incident only by the way, to show the reader the craftiness and cunning of the animal we were dealing with. The only way to get at the wolf would be to come up with a plan, that would take in even that crafty animal. But such a plan, we did not possess, at that point of time.

But let us return to the village of Rupahera and its sarpanch, Roop Singh, who is the hero, or the villain, depending on your fancy, of this particular episode that I wish to narrate. Roop Singh, was a tall, wiry man who possessed a rifle of which he was inordinately proud. This was quite a good rifle, a. 315 ordnance factory weapon, that fired a large steel tipped bullet that could easily account for a tiger at close range. In a region where even a muzzle loader was something of a status symbol, it was natural for Roop Singh to take such pride in his weapon. His only regret was that he got no opportunity to use the gun. Happily that time had now come, and it was his firm resolve to go after the wolf and thus not only rid his village of a dreadful scourge, but also show to the whole tehsil his prowess with a rifle. Roop Singh's plan of action was simple. He procured a strong spot light from Bhopal and positioned himself on top of a hill close to the village. This hill provided a good vantage point and any animal using any of the game trails that ran around the village would be clearly visible from it during the day. During the night the strong spot light could pick out any animal that might be lurking in the vicinity. Roop Singh's plan was therefore quite sensible, all he needed was a dose of luck. *Please walk into my parlour said the spider to the fly* – all he needed was for the wolf to walk into the sights of his gun, and it nearly did.

Not far from the village of Amla Mazzu, and quite close to the track that I have mentioned was a small settlement, consisting of a cluster of eight or nine huts. The inhabitants of this hamlet were *gadariyas* or graziers, who owned a large of herd of milch animals, mostly cows and buffaloes, and made a living by selling this milk. They kept their cattle in large enclosures which were protected by a make shift wooden fence with thorn bushes being wedged in between the horizontal bars for additional safety. It was natural for the man eater to be attracted to these cattle pens, because of the young calves that were to found there, but the graziers kept a sharp look out at night and were well assisted in their vigilance by the fierce bunch of sheep dogs which they kept for guard duties. These sensible precautions that they took, had kept the man eater at bay up till then, and while almost every village had some one to mourn, this small community went about its business, untouched by the hand of tragedy.

Destiny however has its own inscrutable ways of working and just when things appear to be idyllic in their peace and contentment, some unexpected event may suddenly shatter the calm surface of things. So it was here. On the fateful day Sumri, the young daughter of Haricharan, one of the graziers was out cutting grass not far from her hut. Her mother sat near the door of their dwelling, combing her hair and minding the young infant who from to time clamoured for here attentions from within the hut. The afternoon sun slanted down on the pastoral scene. Sumri, a bright and comely girl who was the apple of her parent's eyes, had cut grass to the edge of the Jowar field when suddenly the wolf who had been lying in wait for her in the field, dashed out, grabbed her by the shoulder and disappeared into the thick cover provided by the tall closely growing Jowar crop. Her mother who had witnessed the whole drama, proved that she was not only a brave woman but also had great presence of mind. Picking up a laathi and taking one of the dogs with her she ran after the wolf. The shaggy sheep dog, almost as large as the wolf itself and not less than the wolf in courage, was able to track the wolf and lead the mother to the precise spot where it had taken her daughter. The wolf, which had probably never been pursued so closely or so persistently, took alarm, and leaving the girl in a pool of blood, dashed off into the surrounding forest when its pursuers had closed in on it. The mother found her child, with deep gashes in her shoulder and one of her arms almost severed. Picking up the unconscious child, she brought her quickly to the hut where, still maintaining her composure, she tried to bandage the wounds and stop the flow of blood as best as she could.

As luck would have it, we were quite close to spot where these dramatic events were happening, and the agitated parents were able to stop our jeep as we were proceeding to village Rupahera from Amala Majju. The child was put into a jeep that was following us, and was taken straight to Ashta Hospital, where she was given first aid and then rushed to the medical college at Bhopal. The timely ministrations of the mother and the immediate first aid given to the child not only saved her life, but also obviated the need of amputating her arm. Little Sumri, who must be a grown up lass now, probably a mother herself, can thank her very brave and sensible mother for being alive today.

Sumri was packed off to the hospital with Kaurav, who was following us in his jeep and could be relied upon to mobilise all the resources available at Ashta to save the girl's life. This left us free to turn our attentions to the wolf and to see if could take advantage of the situation. By now the sun had set and day light was fast fading. As the wolf was known to operate only during the day, it was unlikely that we would be able to run into it. However it was just possible that, balked of its kill, it might be induced to take one of the baits that had been put up for it, and it was decided that we should look up these baits and sit up over the one where we thought the wolf was most likely to appear. Towards these baits then we proceeded, driving slowly and also shining the spotlight into the fields and hillsides bordering the road. It may be that the wolf was lurking in one of these places which he was used to frequenting and if he was indeed there, the lights would pick out his eyes, and give us a chance of taking a shot at it.

We had just gone past the spot where the Rupahera road branches off the main track, when we saw the bright eyes of a largish animal in the spotlight. The animal, which we could only see indistinctly before it dashed off into the darkness, appeared to be too large to be a wolf, but then we had seen the man eater and knew it to be well beyond the ordinary in terms of size. It may or may not be the wolf, but it was moving about in an area which was frequented by the wolf, it was roughly the same in size and appearance, and was unlikely to give us a chance of making sure of its identity by closer inspection. As all these thoughts passed through our minds, we had climbed the small gradient that leads the road, by a series of undulations to the top of the Dodi ghat.

We were about mid way up the ghat when we saw the same animal again, running across the road into the darkness towards Rupahera. Siddique, who was with me, was by now sure that the animal which we had seen was indeed the man eater, though I had my doubts. On seeing this creature trotting across the track and running off into the darkness, we turned the jeep off the track and gave chase. The plateau, at this spot, was free from boulders, and it was possible to follow the animal over the firm rolling plain that made up the top of the ghat. The undulating terrain made it possible for us to catch glimpses of the animal whenever it breasted the top of a rise which it did every now and then, before disappearing again into some low lying gully. As I was driving, it was Siddique's turn to take a crack at our quarry and this he did as soon as he saw the wolf cresting the top of a small ridge, about two hundred yards to our left. He was armed on this occasion with a Holland and Holland. 375 magnum rifle, a gun which could bring down an elephant if the shot was accurate, so the range was not a problem. The problem was that this rifle has a vicious kick and its weight makes it hard to hold it steady, and at any rate, to take a shot at a distant target from a moving jeep in uncertain light would have been a difficult undertaking at the best of times. My guess is that, Siddique missed the target.

But now an unexpected complication was introduced into the proceedings. Purely by chance, our chase had taken us, to the exact spot where Roop Singh was sitting up. Alerted by the sound of our jeep and then the report of the single shot fired by Siddique, he realized that the wolf was likely to come into his own line of fire, now was his chance and he was not slow to take it. The problem was, we were also in his line of fire and in his excitement, he was just as likely, probably more likely to hit us than the wolf. This in fact is what almost happened. The sharp report of his powerful rifle reverberated among the hills, as he let loose, first one, then a second shot, both of which, we felt passed quite close to our jeep. We turned our vehicle towards the spot where the shots seem to be coming from and yelled at the top of our voices, asking the Sarpanch to stop firing, but Roop Singh seemed to have sighted the wolf and his blood was up. He let off one more shot, which was followed by a whoop of joy.

By the time we reached Roop Singh he had already emptied the magazine of his rifle and was standing waiting for us, with his rifle grounded and a sheepish grin on his face. Siddique who was fairly worked up by now told the Sarpanch, in choice language that he was guilty of attempted murder, as well certain other grievous offences under the Indian Penal Code. Roop Singh was profuse in his apologies, trying to placate the outraged man of law, not by learned legal arguments but by appealing to his instincts as a shikari. The Sarpanch's defence was that he has sighted a large wolf and like any hunter who at last comes face to face with a quarry that has eluded him so far, he could not restrain himself. Whatever the legal merits of this argument it mollified Siddique sufficiently, for him to suggest that we should continue to look for the wolf, just in case Roop Singh had indeed seen the wolf and wounded the animal. Accordingly we asked Roop Singh to jump into the back of the jeep and lead us to the spot where he thought the animal might be.

Roop Singh did as he was told. Indeed he seemed to be

eager to lead us on to where he thought the wolf was lying dead. He had already made up his mind that the wolf was lying dead somewhere close at hand, and he would soon be a local hero, when the news got around. There were two powerful spot lights in the jeep and Roop Singh and Ram Singh the home guard jawan who has already been alluded to, shone the lights all around as we drove over the desolate plateau. We had not travelled far when Roop Singh asked us to stop the jeep. He had seen a large animal lying in a small depression just off the road, and this is where he led us. At first, as the lights picked out the grey bulk of a largish animal, lying in the small hollow our hopes rose high, but we were in for a disappointment. The animal that Roop Singh had shot, and apparently the animal that we had chased, was not a wolf but a large hyena.

After a brief examination the carcass was handed over to the forest department, who with incredible callousness, threw it on the garbage heap, just outside the range office at Ashta, by the side of the national highway. The inhabitants of that town woke up to find a strange animal lying dead by the roadside, and for a while a crowd of onlookers gathered at the spot, to witness the ignominious fate of wild animal that had perished, for no fault of its own. The man eater had once again given us the slip and continued to terrorize the natives of the neighbouring area.

The bullock cart ride

By now more than a month had passed since the man eater or man eaters first appeared on the scene. During this time more than ten children had lost their lives and countless citizens had lived in dread of the man eater every waking moment of their lives. It is true that we had accounted for one of the animals, which later proved to be a man eater. But this had not made much difference to the killings which seemed to continue unabated. It was clear that we were dealing with a very canny animal and none of the conventional methods of shikar were going to work. It was then that I thought of the bullock cart ride.

The idea was quite simple really, to ride at night in a bullock cart, on the trails most frequented by the man eater. Hitherto we had pursued the man eater by jeep, or lain in wait for it over baits tied up at selected locations. These methods had not worked, probably because the man eater was a very wary animal, unlikely to fall into any simple trap set for it. However if we used a bullock cart rather than a jeep, just as villagers do for moving about, it was unlikely to arouse any suspicion. To make the whole thing appear absolutely natural, we would also have to keep some women and children with us. When this cart moved out, with the women and children chattering merrily, the bells round the necks of the bullocks jingling, no wolf would ever suspect that the cart also held a shikari with a loaded shot gun, waiting for it. A simple but effective plan it seemed to me, but there was only one snag, no women and children would agree to act as decoys, in this manner. But this problem was solved for me in an unexpected way.

As it happened my wife and children had been feeling rather left out of the proceedings ever since the man eater appeared on the scene, because they had not been able to accompany me on tour. On this particular occasion, giving in to the entreaties of my wife, I had allowed them to accompany me to Ashta, strictly on the condition that they would have to stay on in Ashta Rest House, while I was out man eater hunting. This condition was reluctantly accepted, and my wife and two children aged two and four were with me at Ashta when this particular problem arose. I explained the bullock cart plan to my wife and told her how unfortunate it was, that I could not get any women and children to accompany me in the bullock cart, especially since there was really no danger involved. My wife very gamely suggested that she and the children could give me company during the bullock cart ride. She thought it would be a great lark. As I had told her myself that there was no danger involved, I could not very well object. Thus it was that this small problem was circumvented and the stage was set for an experience that proved to be rather more thrilling than I had bargained for.

The *mukaddam* or the Patel of village Rupahera had agreed to put his bullock cart at my disposal, but as he could not get any of his farm labourers to drive the cart he agreed to drive himself. It turned out to be a full moon night, as it always seemed to be whenever we had an encounter with the wolf. The road we had selected was the Rupahera track, from the point where it branches off from the Amla Mazzu road. This track, as has been mentioned before was much frequented by the wolf. A few words about the topography of the place would not be out of place here. The Dodi plateau terminates abruptly in a series of steep headlands, just north of the track. At the foot of these hills is a fairly dense forest of teak, which ends just short of the track. The hills in this part of the world look like the jagged shoreline on a rocky coast, where the sea makes deep indentations in the shape of innumerable small coves and inlets. If you substitute the forest for the sea, you will get the picture. The country to the right of the road is more open and park like, with large trees, standing over the track in places. Beyond this small fringe of open woodland are the fields of jowar, which at that time were ubiquitous in the area.

The *mukkadam* had brought his best cart for us, a neat vehicle, open on the top, with a liberal bedding of straw at the back to cushion the ride. It was drawn by a pair of short but sturdy bullocks, each wearing a tinkling bell round its neck. Leaving our jeep at the junction of the two tracks, we – that is – my wife and two children got on to the bullock cart. My young daughter, who was a mischievous little mite, barely over two years of age, was excited beyond measure at this adventure. Her eyes, which were then round and black as the jamun berries which she was fond of eating, were dancing with excitement. Her brother who was two years older, and therefore already conscious of superior wisdom, was more reserved, but was thrilled nonetheless, but I could already sense that my wife was beginning to have some misgivings about having so readily agreed to my scheme. I did my best to reassure her, telling her that we were not in any danger and asking her to enjoy the lovely scene that was before us.

The landscape before us was indeed a scene of wondrous beauty. The moon shed a flood of radiance on the scene, a radiance which was so white as to be almost blue. I have never seen moonlight like this since then, this light had a glass like transparency, a clear lucent quality, like the clarity of thin ice or a cold clear vein of water cascading over stones in a mountain stream. Every object, every little blade of grass and leaf was etched sharply in the brilliant clarity of that light. There was no wind, it was very still, a deep, mysterious repose seemed to hold everything in a spell. The great trees cast huge shadows on the road, which lay ankle deep in soft white dust.

This spell was broken when our little cart set off, with its bells tinkling and the children prattling excitedly. The driver of our cart, soon launched himself into a rustic song, and what he lacked in tunefulness he seemed to make up in enthusiasm. Disturbed by all this noise, a great horned owl, which was sitting over a stump by the side of the road, flew away noiselessly. Then suddenly the driver seemed to slacken his song. He looked at me with a look of 'wild surmise', yes, I had also heard what he had heard – the distant, but unmistakable sound of a wolf wailing. My wife and children had heard this too, for they suddenly fell silent. The cart went on with its bells tinkling. The wheels raised small puffs of dust, which fell back after dancing in the moonlight for a while. The silence seemed to return again like the tide returning.

I kept a sharp lookout over the small stockade that enclosed the back of the cart. But the wolf after his initial call was keeping quiet. The small jungle sounds that engage your attention while sitting up over a kill could not be heard over the noise of the cart. After a while the spell was broken, the children started chattering again and our cart driver again started humming a song under his breath, he was still too chastened to sing. A nightjar rose suddenly, out of a small depression in the road where he was sitting, all but invisible. Some people consider this bird, a bird of ill omen, and I was wondering what will happen when suddenly the silence of the night was once again shattered, this time by the scream of a human being in agony. The scream seemed to come from the right of the road. It was not repeated, but there was no doubt that it seemed to come from a person in mortal fear of his life. The scream appeared to come from the direction of a small temple, that stands in a dense grove just south of the road, about five hundred yards from where we were. Shouting at the top of my voice to the person, who was apparently in danger, I told him that help was at hand and he should hang on for just a moment. I then asked my cart driver to push his bullocks as hard as he could. This he did and the sturdy little animals, broke into a fast trot, arriving at the temple in a lather of sweat in just a few minutes.

This temple was a simple whitewashed structure, dedicated to shiva. It stood on a broad platform, that was built all around it. This temple was looked after by a sadhu, a mendicant who has renounced the world. This sadhu was actually a young man, with long matted locks and intense brooding eyes. He was a silent, reclusive person, and I suspect the villagers were in awe of him. As the temple was too small for anyone to sleep inside, the sadhu used to sleep on the platform. The only concession to the cold weather he would make was a small fire which he kept burning by his side. Otherwise a thin sheet of cotton, was his only raiment and covering, hot weather or cold. A true ascetic was this young man, who had forsaken the world at this youthful age to pursue the call of his spirit. When we reached the temple, the sadhu was sitting up on the platform with blood flowing profusely from his left shoulder. The fire that he always kept burning had burned down to a few smouldering embers. This was the story that I got out of him.

"As you know sahib, it is my practice to sleep outside, whether it is winter or summer. I fear no man, and no animal certainly. Yes! I had heard about this wolf, and have even heard it calling in the forest many a times, but what has a sadhu to fear from an animal. But this animal must be a powerful evil spirit, because only such spirits can harm a sadhu. Sahib as I was sleeping, I felt a tearing pain in my shoulders and I must have screamed out involuntarily. This was the scream you heard. Inspite of the pain, my eyes opened instantly and I was alert, for a sadhu's sleep is light. I saw this big wolf with its fangs buried in my shoulder. I picked up the tongs, which I always keep at my side and took out a burning ember from my fire and thrust it at the wolf's muzzle. With a snarl of rage, the wolf loosened its hold on my shoulder. Just then I heard your shout. The wolf must have heard it too, because he then disappeared into the darkness as suddenly as he had come. I tell you sahib, this is no animal, but a spirit, but I am also a sadhu, and though he can harm me, he can not yet kill me."

As he told me his story, the sadhu must have been in considerable pain, but if he was, he did not show it. His eyes still burned with a fiery intensity. He scouted my suggestions that he come with me to Ashta for treatment. He assured me, that he had his own medicine which was more effective that any thing that we could provide. As the sadhu was thus resolved, not to leave his temple, or to take treatment outside, we decided to leave him where he was. But one thing we did, we helped him build up a large fire from a heap of firewood that was kept nearby. This fire would keep the wolf at bay, if he was lurking nearby. I raised a silent salute to a very brave man, and turned to get back to our cart to begin our return journey, but a complication now arose. The mukkadam said, his bullocks were too tired after their sprint, to immediately be put to harness again. They would have to rested overnight before we could return. The choice before me was thus, either to stay on and spend the rest of the night at the temple, or brave the return journey on foot. I chose to go back. Nothing could however induce the mukkadam to go with us. He preferred to lock himself up inside the temple and spend the night doubled up like a sack, rather than brave the imagined dangers of the road.

So there was nothing for it us but to take to the road on our own. This was not such a foolhardy undertaking as it seems. I knew the wolf would never attack a party of four which included an armed man. As long as we kept to the middle of the track and kept a sharp lookout, we should be absolutely safe. My wife and children were fortunately of the same mind, they thought nothing of walking back, they knew they would not be in any real danger, so long as we remained alert. So we set off on our return journey, my wife leading, the two kids in the middle and I at the back.

The journey was not a long one, the night was beautiful, the road stretched ahead, with the jungle on one side and the large trees on the other. The moon still shone overhead, large, resplendent, shedding its flood of vitreous light on the whole scene. Much as I love nature however, I could not really enjoy its beauty because I had to keep my senses tuned to the task in hand. Our feet made no noise on the soft sand, the jungle was silent, but I could sense that the wolf was watching us. I fancied that I saw the gleam of eyes, glaring, baleful and red, following us in the darkness. We had been on the road about half an hour when a fox, darted across, from the right, raising a flurry of dust in his wake, and startling all of us. When we came to the tree stump, we saw that the large owl was back on his perch. This time he did not rise at our approach, but kept looking down at us with that brooding mournfulness that owls have

By now our journey was nearly over. The two children had regained their spirits by now.They were laughing and clapping as they saw our jeep standing in the fork of the road, with Shamshad the driver and Ram Singh the Home Guard Jawan waiting for us. As the driver turned the ignition and the jeep roared to life we heard it again, at first almost inaudible, then slowly in volume, a curious but unmistakable sound, like the wind soughing among the trees ; it was the wolf throwing us his challenge again.

Shahjade makes his appearance

You will remember the various arrangements we had made for killing the wolf. Baits had been tied up at select locations and forest department sharpshooters had been put into carefully made hides over game trails that were most frequented by the wolf. SAF marksmen were patrolling the area round the clock and mounting guard over vulnerable villages. All these sensible precautions had however not yielded any results. The lone wolf that we had succeeded in killing, was due to the jungle craft of the Pardhis, but even they had not been lucky again. It was at this juncture that we were approached by a group of shikaris, headed by a gentleman who went by the royal name of Shahjade or the prince.

Shahjade made a favourable impression on me, and what impressed me most was his beautiful rifle. This was an ordnance factory. 315 rifle, the same as Roop Singh's rifle, but there the resemblance ended. Shajade's weapon was beautifully blued with a gleaming walnut stock. The rifle had a silver foresight and a precisely calibrated back sight. Shajade was a obviously a hunter who took a great deal of pains over the accuracy and upkeep of his weapon and such a man was probably a good shikari as well. I had no hesitation in permitting him to join the hunt, the only condition that I made was that he must confine his activities to the Arnia Ghazi plateau so as not to run the risk of running into others also looking for the wolf. This condition was readily accepted and Shajade thus became an important member of our party.

One afternoon as D'cruz and I were having tea in the veranda of the Dodi Rest House, we were surprised to see a jeep enter the Rest House at a great speed and come to a screeching halt just in front of us. From the jeep alighted Shahjade and a venerable old gentlemen with a flowing white beard. D'cruz and I were invited to inspect the contents of the jeep, with great ceremony, by the old gentleman who conducted us to the back of the jeep and with a flourish removed a cloth that was covering its floor. A startling sight then met our eyes.

Lying on the floor of the jeep, was a young lamb, its stomach slit open and by the side of the lamb lay a large wolf, with blood still trickling from its muzzle. This wolf was a very old and large animal, its fur was scanty, and what there was had turned a pale yellow. It was as large as a large Alsatian dog, but looked much more fierce. There was no doubt in any one's mind that before us lay the man eater, or one of the man eaters of Ashta. The rest of the story is best told in Shahjade's own words.

"I have, as you know shot many animals in my time. I have dealt with man eating tigers and leopards. There was a man eating tiger in Bastar which had wrought havoc in timber camps during the felling operations. I put a stop to its depredations. I have even faced a rouge elephant. I have an elephant gun, a double barrelled Rigby rifle, which I haven't brought with me here. This elephant was operating somewhere down south, in the foothills of the Nilgiri mountain, I forget which state it was, because Tamil Nadu and Karnataka have a common border there. This elephant was so feared that even the sandalwood poachers had run away from the forest. I was then engaged by the forest department to deal with it."

"I came face to face with it when it was in the process of trampling down a Toda's hut. It came at me with an angry bellow but I put two heavy bullets between its eyes, and it went down as if pole axed. I know how animals behave, how they operate, but I tell you sir! I have not come across any animal as cunning as this. I will tell you what happened when I was once sitting up at a waterhole waiting for the wolf. I was sitting with my back to a rock, when I heard a stealthy rustle, behind me. This was strange, because the game trail which led to the waterhole ran in front of me. All other animals had approached the water from the front, but for some reason the wolf was circling the waterhole and approaching the water from the back. As I was sitting directly in its line of approach, it must have got wind of me. For after a while, I heard a wolf howling, almost half a mile away, behind me. I realised that I was dealing with a cunning devil and I would have to set aside all my experience and knowledge and come up with something new when dealing with this animal."

"Well! as you know it is my practice to patrol the Arnia Gazi plateau during the day. I was following the same routine today, when I saw a shepherd, whom I knew, running hard towards me. The shepherd told me that the wolf had just killed one of his lambs and if we made haste, we might find the wolf still at the kill and possibly get a shot at it. I asked the man to jump in and lead us to the spot. After hard driving for about five minutes, the man pointed to the right and showed us where the wolf was standing up over the kill, about three hundred yards away."

"There were now two options before us, I could try to approach closer to get a better shot at the wolf, or I could take my chances from where we were. I asked Mamu here to continue driving slowly so as not to alarm the wolf. At the same time I took aim and fired at the wolf. It was a hurried shot, taken from a moving jeep, but for some reason I knew that I would not miss the target. At the shot the wolf toppled over and fell over the kill, and just to make sure I sent in a quite unnecessary second shot to follow the first."

That, sir! is how we got the man eating wolf of Ashta, and as I knew you were staying at the Rest House with the S.P saab, we decided to drive down here straight away and give you the glad tidings."

That was how the man eater of Ashta, or at least one of the animals met its end. In return for the excellent work that Shahjade had done, he made an unusual request. He wanted to be appointed a Sub Inspector in the police. I sent his request to the Home department, where it was promptly turned down by the babus and the burra babus sitting in the secretariat. The state police, it seemed, did not want any one on its rolls who could shoot straight.

A duck shooting interlude

After shooting down the wolf, it was natural for complacency to set in. We all thought, we had done a wonderful job, and there would be no more kills henceforth. But as usual we were in for a rude shock. Only two days later a child was killed in village Gwala about ten kilometres away. It was clear that though we had accounted for another member of the pack, the man eater, or at least one of the man eaters, possibly the leader of the pack was still alive and well.

We had now been on the trail of the elusive animal for more than a month, and though I did not lack for creature comforts, the sense of failure and a feeling of despair was beginning to creep into our party. To relieve the tension, we decided to take a break from man eater hunting and spend some time at our favourite sport, duck shooting.

I think it may be in order to say a few words about shot guns which play such an important role in duck shooting. These come in various shapes and sizes and often reflect the personality of their owners. Some like double barrelled guns, some single barrelled ones. Some favour the long barrelled gun, others prefer the shorter regulation size. The most prized shot guns are those made by the British firm Purdy, now sadly no longer in business. Purdies often come in pairs and have the same snob value among gun owners, as Rolls Royces have among car owners. After Purdy come the Holland and Holland shot guns, made by the British gunmaker of the same name. Italian Berettas are also much prized and lately Spanish guns have also entered the lists in a big way. A good shot gun is a thing of beauty, with a polished walnut stock, suitably embellished with carving and a gun metal blue lightweight barrel that is no less beautiful. The fancier guns may have silver chasing on the trigger guard and engraving on the breech. The newer models are gas operated and can shoot several shells, one after the other. However in this matter, as in so many others, I am a traditionalist, and I favour the hand loaded single or double barrelled gun over its modern counterpart.

Shooting is a sport, and there is no sport in firing a whole cannonade at a defenceless animal. The well placed single shot, that brings down the quarry, is what all hunters aspire to, and for this the self restraint imposed by the older weapons, is preferable any day, to the self indulgence of the new automatic weapons.

Unfortunately, though a lover of guns, the only shot gun that I have ever possessed is a humble ordnance factory weapon, crude, heavy and entirely lacking in finish. What it lacks in elegance though, it makes up in effectiveness, and has been a faithful companion in many a shoot. Dr Haidar, on the other hand, possessed a light weight Spanish single barrel gun, which he claimed possessed extraordinary accuracy and range. I do not recall the details of Siddique's gun, but like everything about the man it was accurate and efficient.

The destination of choice, when ever we went out shooting ducks, was Bhagwanpura tank. Situated about ten kilometres from the district town of Sehore, this tank is a stretch of clear blue water at the head of rich farming country. The lake is shaped like a seven pointed star, with the seven arms terminating in narrow winding creeks, where at the extremity, the channel is narrow enough for a man to jump across. These creeks, are the perfect places for sitting up for ducks, because they offer enough cover for a hunter to conceal himself and because the ducks like to feed among the weeds that grow at the shore line in these creeks.

There are two methods of shooting ducks. The more commonly employed method depends on the use of decoys.

These are made of either wood or rubber and often look surprisingly like real ducks. When these are not available, even a few pieces of paper scattered on the ground can do the trick. Decoys work because, ducks like to come down where they see other birds already sitting. Ducks are extremely wary, and they normally post sentries to watch for trouble, when they are out feeding. It is almost impossible to surprise them, but the decoys lull them into a false sense of security and thus make it possible for the cautious hunter to surprise them.

The other method, can work only when there are two tanks situated in close proximity of each other. If this happens to be the case, then two guns are sent out to flush the birds from one of the tanks. This is easily accomplished by firing a few shots at the birds, as they sit in the middle of the water. Thus disturbed the birds rise and head for the nearest body of water, in this case the other tank, where, carefully concealed, the hunters are already lying in wait for them. Their 'hide', is usually directly under the flight path of the approaching ducks. As the birds come down to alight on the water, they are fired upon by the hunters while still in the air, and this method usually succeeds in bringing down at least a few birds.

However on this day we chose neither of these methods. Dr Haidar, was the progenitor of a rather new idea, which seemed to appeal to all of us because of its very novelty. Close to the shoreline at Bhagwanpura tank, was an old boat, a fisherman's dory, that had been for years, lying on its keel near the banks, and was now buried almost upto the gunwales in soft mud. Dr Haidar's idea, like most ideas emanating from his fertile mind, was bold in conception, but difficult in execution. He wanted us to unearth the boat, row it to the middle of the lake, and after concealing ourselves in it, wait for the birds. This we now proceeded to do. It was not difficult to free the boat from the encrusting mud, but devising a suitable oar took a little more time. Finally a small *zareba* was made out by cutting down enough ipoemia bushes and arranging them over the boat. In this stockade we concealed ourselves, waiting for what seemed like hours for the ducks to arrive. The boat kept bobbing gently on the placid waters of the lake, but no birds arrived. Evidently our hide was not as good as we thought, or the birds had seen us at work and were therefore keeping away. Whatever the reason, Dr Haidar's bright idea, did not seem so bright in retrospect.

But perhaps it was just as well that they did not do so. Frankly, I do not think I had the heart for shooting ducks. A few months later I gave up this sport altogether, and have not touched a gun ever since, except once to scare away monkeys who were damaging my wheat crop. Ducks are, after all, beautiful creatures. Any one who has seen a duck at close quarters will know what I mean. Their downy plumage has the most beautiful variegated colours, their brilliantly coloured speculum and their proud carriage gives them a special cachet. Who says ducks waddle! they have the imperious grace of a queen. A concourse of ducks, wild teals, brilliantly coloured mallards, the proud sheldrake, the sprightly pintails and the ultimate prize that all hunters seek ;the bar headed goose; is a delightful sight when they float on the waters. Unfortunately the only duck that most people see is a dead duck. Therefore it wasn't such a tragedy after all that we did not kill any ducks that day.

As the ducks had proved elusive, we decided to round off the day's sport by a spot of grouse shooting. By grouse I mean, sand grouse of course. These birds are also distinctive creatures. When in flight they utter a peculiar double call, a short sharp guttural sound, which gives away their position to any observer on the ground. They usually come down to drink water when the sun has already been up for some hours. When they alight, they do so in a row, and after coming down they sit still for a while, watching the scene carefully, and looking for all the world, like a row of meditating monks. Once they have satisfied themselves that there is no danger in sight, they walk up to the water, one step at a time. Each step is followed by a pause, and a careful reconnaissance. Their plumage blends so perfectly with the earth, that one might easily mistake one for a clod or a stone

That morning, the sand grouse had come down in an area where the ground was gently undulating. Intersecting this terrain of small dunes were channels of water, the creeks and inlets described above. The problem was, just as we peeped over the crest of one dune the birds would spot us and fly away to the next dune. After repeating this process, two or three times, we finally gave up. It seemed we would just have to wait for our luck to turn.

Next morning we decided to set out early, before the sun

was up. Our destination this time was the Jamonia irrigation tank. This is a large tank, situated a few miles west of Sehore. This tank is distinguished from Bhagwanpura, and indeed other tanks of the kind, by a dense growth of vegetation at the margin of the lake. This vegetation affords good cover for hunters and the tank is therefore ideal for duck shooting. What makes it special is the fact that the comparatively heavier cover provides the hunter with some chance of getting a shot at that most wary bird of all, the Siberian goose.

We – that is Siddique, Dr Haider and myself – were at the tank early next morning. It was quite chilly thus early in the day, and the dew lay thick on the green, damp, sward that fringed the margin of the lake. The tank was nearly full, which made it difficult for us to reach across to the far side, where the ducks prefer to feed early in the day. If we chose to walk around to other side, it would mean making a huge circuit that might take the better part of an hour and we would lose precious time in the process. Dr Haider suggested that we could get over to the other side by a short cut which was jeepable, but only just. As no one else seemed to know anything about this path Dr Haider was asked to take the wheel.

The next few minutes were exhilarating, as Dr Haider, after lighting a cigarette and putting it between his lips, sent the old Ford jeep careering over ditches and potholes and through clumps of bushes and stretches of water that appeared to almost knee deep in places. When I asked him how he managed to steer the vehicle when no kind of path was visible, he told me that before the tank was constructed there used to be a well worn cart track around the tank, and as he had spent his youth in these parts, he remembered this track and was able to steer along quite nicely on this basis. I fervently hoped that his memory would prove to be more accurate in this one instance than it usually was in other cases, and when we arrived at a patch of dry ground on the far side of the tank, I raised a small prayer of thanksgiving. Siddique who had been sweating rather too much, given the cold weather, now lit his pipe with ostentatious nonchalance. Our amphibious journey had taken us less than ten minutes.

Having arrived at our destination in good time, with the faint crimson tinge of dawn barely beginning to be visible over the eastern horizon, we were soon in position behind clumps of densely growing bushes. Siddique had suggested that we divide our forces, each one taking a separate position, but Dr Haider elected to stay with me, while Siddique took up his stand a little distance away where he thought he had a better chance of getting a shot. Siddique had so positioned himself, that he would be able to get the first shot at the ducks, and as one shot was all that we would be able to get, if we stayed where we were, we had hardly any chance of adding anything to our bag. After whispered consultation with Dr Haider we decided to shift our base a few hundred yards to the left, where the cover was less thick, but there was just the odd chance that if Siddique fired and missed, some stragglers might alight close to us and give us a chance. After squelching through the soggy turf for another ten minutes we were installed in our new hide and sat down to await developments.

Dr Haider, who was growing more and more excited with the passage of time, now took out his handkerchief, a after fashioning it in the shape of what he claimed was a duck, he placed it the edge of the water just in front of our hide. This he told me was an infallible ploy to attract the biggest prize of duck shooting, the grey lag goose or – *Kaz* – as he called it. When he said the word, 'kaz' he said it with a kind of hushed reverence. Today, he said, he had a hunch that we were going to get this bird. The grey light of dawn had by now completely dissipated and a beautiful winter sunrise had flooded the lake and the mist wrapped shoreline with clear lucent light. The lake was calm as glass. It was just the kind of weather that the ducks like and we could see far away in the centre of the lake, large contingents of ducks detach themselves from the main body, like large ships leaving the harbour and head for the shoreline. After a while we heard a shot from Siddique, after a few seconds this was followed by another shot. The birds that he had scared away rose up in compact body after circling overhead for a longish while, a large covey of birds came down just where Dr Haider had placed his handkerchief as decoy. I raised my gun and was about to fire, but Dr Haider motioned to me to wait. I held my fire and waited. Sure enough, after a few moments, a large bird with a wonderful mottled plumage landed close to us. As it did so Dr Haider, very sportingly waived his own chance and asked me to take the shot. The large bird, so close to our guns was an easy target, literally a sitting duck, and it was an easy thing to put a load of buck shot into it. As the dripping bird was retrieved by Ram Singh, there was no happier man than the good doctor, whose self denial had given me a chance to bag the goose.

The Commissioner arrives

All through this incident the Commissioner at Bhopal was Satyam, and he was a tower of strength to all of us, who were his official subordinates. Satyam was an officer of the old school, a vanishing breed today. He was a man of middling height, bespectacled, with a prominent nose and a sharp clean shaven face. In his personal life he was a Spartan, as so many of our best officers have been. He always wore a simple cotton bush shirt, cold weather or hot, did not smoke or drink and partook of other stimulants only sparingly. He had a commanding intellect ; I have never found any one who was so quick to seize the essentials of any problem, however involved it might have been. Satyam had a quick temper, he was also opinionated and vain and was apt to be rather too polite before important people, but these are small faults, if they can be called faults at all. They are as nothing when set beside his virtues, his inflexible rectitude, his ascetic personal life, and his unswerving support and loyalty to his subordinates.

Satyam realised, at an early stage in the proceedings, that the best thing he could to help us in dealing with the problem, was not to interfere in the field operations. This was indeed a wise policy. Unlike so many of the busybodies sitting in the Secretariat, he realised that being away from the scene of action, whatever advice and guidance that he could offer was bound to be divorced from reality and therefore off the mark. He contented himself therefore, by asking me frequently for status reports and encouraging us in our efforts, in whatever way he could. However a complication now arose. The minister incharge of the district, let us call him Bansilal, a stout well rounded gentleman, who was always dressed in neatly starched white Kurtas and payjamas, wished to visit the affected area and see things for himself. It was understood that the Minister's visit would be a ceremonial one in the sense that the he would visit some bereaved families, give a few pep talks to the assembled villagers to put heart into them and then leave. It would thus be a mere formality and Satyam would insure that the Minister stuck to his itinerary.

Thus it was that on the appointed day the Minister's motorcade swept down the Indore road with a great deal of fanfare. The Minister was in a white Ambassador car, with a starched tricolor flying on the bonnet and a red beacon light on the top. His entourage included two other cars carrying his staff. This fleet of official cars with all the accoutrements of authority made an impressive display, but it was quite useless if the intention was to visit the interior areas where the wolf was operating. As the Minister was quite keen to visit one village in the interior where the wolf had claimed some victims, I offered to put the Minister and Commissioner in my own jeep and drive them round. The Minister's body guard, along with my own Home Gurad Jawan, Ram Singh I put in Kaurav's jeep, which followed us at a small distance.

I was driving on the Amal Mazzu road, intending to detour to Pardhikhera, and introduce the Minister to my friend Raja Ram Pardhi, who had played such a notable part in the story. The track in those days was a rough up and down affair and a jeep, after all is a vehicle for covering distance, not for comfort. The Minister because of his bulk, was wedged in between Satyam and me, with the gear shift almost jammed between his legs. Whenever I had to change gear, I had to step on the Minister's toes, so that he would open out his legs. Satyam, who was aware of the Minister's discomfiture, added quite gratuitously,"be careful Yadav!, we have a VIP on board."

Driving down this road, with which I was by now thoroughly familiar, I kept one eye on track, looking for pug marks. The soft dust on the road provided an excellent surface for these and fortunately, just as we were closing in on the village of Pardhikhera, I saw the fresh pug marks of the wolf, imprinted clearly in the dust. I pointed this out to Satyam and the Minister. I also said that the pug marks were quite fresh, which showed that the wolf was some where close by and there was a possibility, albeit a remote one, that we just might run into it. This brought about an immediate change in the Minister's manner, he became nervous and fidgety and started worrying whether, it would not be wiser if I went after the wolf, without two non-combatant passengers tagging along, so to speak. I told the Minister, that his presence would not be a serious impediment, indeed, he may be able to give valuable advice in the matter, but he would not listen. He made me stop the jeep and asked the Commissioner to disembark, as well. Satyam had no choice but to keep the Minister the company. Both these worthies, thus got off the jeep, close to the village of Pardhikhera and bade me go after the wolf.

By now Kaurav's jeep had caught up with us and he was asked to take the Minister to the nearby village of Pardhikhera. I asked Ram Singh to join me, but the Minister's body guard who carried a sten gun also insisted on jumping in. Obviously, his sten gun had given him the illusion that he was also a Shikari. This was in fact a dangerous illusion, a sten gun is a defensive weapon. It can fire with great rapidity, is extremely light and has a short barrel. All of which makes it a formidable self defence weapon. But in Shikar, where the hunter may be required to fire at a distant and fast moving target, accuracy is more important than firepower. A stengun in such a situation is worse than a sling. All these thoughts occurred to me as the Minister's body guard got into the jeep but it was useless to argue with him. When a man is armed with a sten gun, he thinks he is invincible and rationality may not have any impact on him.

Pardhikhera is a small village and news of the arrival of VIPs had already reached the villagers, who had collected in a body on a small knoll, near the village to wait for the Minister's party. I was about to turn my jeep and head off in the direction of Amal Mazzu, where I thought it was more likely that the wolf might be, when a couple of small boys came running up to the knoll shouting, bagherra, bagherra, and pointing in the direction of Rupahera, down a well worn but barely serviceable cart track. I turned my jeep in the direction pointed out and we were in pursuit, before the crowd had had enough time to react. I knew that if the Pardhis went after the wolf, with their ancient matchlocks and muzzle loaders, they would put paid to what ever chance there might be of my bagging the wolf. The Pardhis are unbeatable as trappers of game, but they have no notion of hunting with a rifle or shot gun. For this reason I wanted to put as much distance as possible between my jeep and the group of excited tribesmen.

The track that we were following was a very rough one, deeply rutted and dotted with small boulders which made the going difficult. After passing over open country for a while, the track entered a narrow defile where it passed between two hills. These hills are really outcrops of black basaltic rock, covered on the top with a thin coating of soil. Their sides were bare of vegetation and the defile was a bleak and melancholy place. This defile terminates abruptly and one then enters a wide amphitheatre, bounded with low hills, whose floor is a stony lava plane, through the middle of which runs a little stream. This lava plain is bare of vegetation, like the hills which surround it, in fact not a blade of grass can one discern in the whole desolate landscape which opens out before one. This stark landscape is not without a wild beauty of its own, if one has eyes to see it. It was my guess that the wolf was making for this lava plain, and as I entered it, I stopped the jeep and reconnoitred the whole plain slowly, inch by inch. As I did so, my scrutiny was rewarded by the sight of two tiny specks running in the distance, which according to my reckoning were a pair of wolves.

There were now two options open before me. I could give chase to the animals, and try for a shot, if I could get close enough to fire. Or I could make a detour and position myself at the far end of the lava plain, where a similar defile led away from the amphitheatre. If I chose the first option it was likely that the wolf would be alerted and make off before I could get close enough to get in a shot. The second option was obviously more promising, but there was the chance that the wolf or wolves, might not follow the route I expected them to take. It was quite possible that they might turn back and exit from the same route which I had been following upto now. There were also many caves in the hills surrounding the lava plain and the animals might be heading for one of these caves. On balance however the second option seemed to offer the best chance and I decided to take it.

The only way to cut off the retreating animals was to retrace our way out of the lava plain and then after turning east make a detour round the hills which formed the eastern fringe of the amphitheatre. This meant taking the jeep cross country over terrain where there was no track of any kind. The jeep I was driving was a standard four wheel drive Mahindra, and it proved that there is nothing in India to beat it for rough driving. We were following a barely defined game trail that was not more than a yard wide even in the best places. For long periods the trail completely disappeared and we were forced to make our way over bare hard baked earth that was strewn with boulders and broken up into small gullies and ravines scoured out by rain. It was the kind of landscape that gives nightmare to rally drivers. After bumping along somehow for a while, we came to a deep crevice with precipitous sides which could not be crossed by the jeep. We still had to cover about half a kilometre, but if we wanted to cover it, we would have to complete the rest of the journey on foot. So we got off the jeep and all three of us, Ram Singh, the Minister's body guard and I broke into a run, trying to make the end of the defile before the wolves did.

I had done some cross country running in school, but had given up the sport, finding it far too strenuous for my limited reserves of energy. The passage of years had done nothing to improve my stamina and wind, and I was running with a rifle on my back, which added to my difficulties. No wonder I found the going hard. By the time we reached the defile I was gasping for breath. Ram Singh was comparatively in better shape, but the Minister's gun man was also badly winded. This defile was similar to the one I have described earlier, but much wider. The low hills which bordered the lava plain, had come together here like the two arms of a pincer, leaving but a small gap between them. This gap was the defile which provided the only means of egress from a natural enclosure. The lava plain and the defile were completely bare of any vegetation and this meant we would have to conceal ourselves by lying flat on the ground behind a small boulder. As the boulder did not provide good cover, we would also have to keep completely still and also hold our fire, until we were completely sure of hitting the wolf. All these thoughts were passing through my mind and I was just about to brief the other two men with me, when we saw, two small black spots bobbing up and down over the plain in the middle distance. The wolves were coming.

All of us lay still and waited. The two animals came closer and we could see the big wolf, accompanied by a smaller one coming towards us at a steady trot. But the wolf is a wary animal. Just as they were about a hundred and fifty yards the animals halted, the big wolf sniffing the wind and taking stock, by scanning the terrain in front of him inch by inch. The wind was blowing from the wolf towards us, so I knew that the wolf would not be able to detect us, if we lay perfectly still. I held my fire and lay still. The smaller wolf, for some reason, was looking back over its shoulder and giving every appearance of being restless. He appeared in fact to be turning back, but I knew that it would follow the big wolf. My companion, the gun man however thought otherwise, and at this point fired a volley of shots from the sten gun at the wolves. He obviously thought that by peppering the ground in front of him, he would make up for the lack of accuracy of his weapon and probably bring down the wolf. This was a silly mistake. The animals were well outside the range of his gun and, whether he fired one shot or hundred, the chances of hitting the animals remained the same. The shots fired by the gun man raised a shower of splinters from the hard stony ground, and had there been any one about, the ricochet from the random firing might have proved dangerous. Fortunately for all of us, the place was completely deserted for miles. At the shots both the wolves whipped around and went dashing away, the same way that they had come. Here was another chance wasted by a trigger happy policeman, who should have known better. The wolves would continue their depredations, as their time had not yet come. But I was prepared to bide my time. I knew the time would come, when providence would be on the side of the hunter rather than the hunted. Until then one had to wait.

An unaccountable incident

There is a village road that runs from Amarpura to Amal Mazzu, which was much frequented by the man eater. This is a broad dusty track down the side of which there is a line of lantana bushes running along like a verge, for quite a distance. The pug marks of the wolf were often seen on the soft dust of this track. This track is a sort of rural thoroughfare and was much used by bullock carts during the hours of daylight. But as soon as darkness fell it became deserted and one could look down the road for quite a distance in both the directions with an uninterrupted view. My reasoning was that if the wolf was using this track, as he evidently was, then we should be able to get a clear shot at it, whenever it came walking down the track, if we concealed ourselves in the bushes that grew down the side of the road.

Close to the spot we selected for sitting up was a ruined hut that had belonged to a shepherd boy. This boy was an orphan who lived in the hut with his cows and buffaloes as his only companions. One day, the villagers found the animals wandering about the hut without the boy who was always to be found with them. This was most unusual, because every one knew that the boy was extremely fond of his animals and it was totally out of character for him to leave his animals untended, unfed and unwatered. A search was started. The hut was found to empty, the bed not slept in. Nor was there any sign of the boy in the neighbourhood. He had apparently disappeared without a trace. As there were no relatives to grieve over the matter or to pursue it further, the incident was soon forgotten and the animals that were found on the spot were simply taken away by the villagers and divided up among themselves. This incident, I gathered, had occurred just before the first human kill of the man eater of Ashta was recorded.

Although only two months had passed since this incident, the hut was already a desolate ruin. The only door had been removed by vandals and now the open portals formed a gaping hole. The walls were crumbling and the rooftree about to fall.

The rough country tiles which covered the rafters had been blown off, here and there, by the wind. The cattle pen adjacent to the house had been all but demolished by the same forces of nature and what was left had been taken away by thieves. A rank growth of grass and weeds grew copiously, both without and within this forsaken dwelling. The utter dilapidation of this hut, which had once been home to a human being and a score of animals, and the sad story connected with it was enough to produce the most melancholy train of thoughts. These sombre thoughts must have been in mind when, we took up our station.

As we sat down in our hide, a large gibbous moon was rising. Our hide had been prepared by hollowing out the middle of a cluster of lantana bushes. We, that is Dr Haidar and I, had hoped for a comfortable evening sitting in this enclosure, but we had reckoned without the innumerable little insects that started crawling into our clothes, and biting us in all over the exposed parts of our bodies, as soon as it was dark. A light wind arose, as the night advanced, and the dust rose from the road in small swirls and eddies, before falling back. Waiting for a crafty animal to show itself, in such a situation, is a game of patience, but this night proved to be a sore trial, even for my usually monumental patience. For a while I watched the great concourse of stars, wheeling in the inverted bowl of the sky. The constellation Orion, was directly overhead, and the red star that makes up the warrior's eye in Orion seemed to be burning with peculiar fire. The moonlight on this occasion seemed faint and wan. As the hours dragged by Dr Haidar fell into a doze. I sat on, enduring the insects and the growing monotony of the interminable vigil.

But suddenly, I think it must have been a little past three in the morning, I felt my senses tingle. A blast of cold air seemed to come from the direction of the hut, and I felt completely awake. I had a premonition of something about to happen, but what, I could not say. The road stretched ahead as before, empty and deserted. Then with an unexpectedness that was shocking the silence was shattered, by a scream, a human scream, that seemed to come from somewhere in front of the hut. The scream, had a high pitched quaver, like the voice of an adolescent. It was not repeated, but there was no doubt in my mind that I heard a human being, possibly a young lad, screaming for dear life. However Dr Haidar, continued to doze as before, it was clear that he had heard nothing.

I left my hide to investigate, feeling a little foolish, because from where I sat I could see the entire road, for nearly half a kilometre, as well as the ruined hut, and no human being could have come within earshot without showing himself. I walked around the hut as well as the surrounding area, but of course there was nothing, no footmarks, or any other signs of the presence of any other being, man or beast, anywhere. I could find no rational explanation for what I had heard, yet I could not discount the evidence of my senses. I had clearly heard, the unmistakable ;piteous, and most melancholy sound of a human being screaming at the last extremity of his life. I consider myself a sensible, pragmatic person, but the explanation of this event that I have worked out, and which I will put before the reader at the end of this book, calls for a simple acceptance of "things that are not dreamt of in your philosophy".

The rest of the night, after this incident passed quickly. I awakened Dr Haidar and asked him what, if he had heard anything. He had heard nothing. He told me, that when I woke him up he was dreaming of shooting the wolf, which had just walked into his carefully laid trap. He was about to take aim and fire, when I had disturbed him so unnecessarily. But Dr Haidar, being a diehard optimist, interpreted this as a good omen. He had a theory that in real life events often followed the opposite course from dreams. So by his reckoning we were now slated for a successful encounter with the wolf. When I told him about the scream that I had heard, he thought it must have been my overwrought imagination. For the time being I had no option but to agree with him.

Realising that our vigil would not now be fruitful, we enjoyed a quiet smoke, and just as dawn was breaking, set off in our jeep for Ashta Rest House, to rest, and be ready again to pit our wits against the man eater.

A review of the situation

We had been pursuing the man eater now for almost two months, with some mixed luck. But of late, but for Shahjade's unexpected success, we had nothing to show for the effort we had put in. It was therefore time to take stock, to review our strategy, and if necessary to effect changes in it. Accordingly we decided to hold another council of war.

This was held, as before, in the Dodi Rest House. D'cruz of whom I have spoken before, as well as senior officers of the forest department were in attendance. This review came up with some valuable suggestions and its worth summarising its conclusions.

Our first mistake we felt, was that right from the start, we had assumed that the man eater was a lone wolf, a single animal, very much above the average in size, strength and cunning. There are obvious reasons why such a theory appealed to all concerned. To begin with we were influenced by the information that was available about man eating tigers and leopards, where the man eater is usually a single animal. Our basic source of information about man eating tigers and wolves are the stories of Jim Corbett, and he always wrote about either single man eaters or at worst a pair of tigers, where the second animal was usually a grown up cub that had become a man eater in the company of its mother. His famous story about the man eating leopard of Rudraprayag, deals with the exploits of a single animal of diabolical cunning and craftiness. This animal had established a reign of terror in the whole of upper Alaknanda and Mandakini valleys for several years, and had the reputation of being possessed of almost supernatural cunning. It was finally shot by Corbett, over a bait, not far from the town of Rudraprayag. His other famous stories, like the story of the Chowgarh tiger and the Thak man eater, are all about the doings of single tigers, where the hunter is called upon to match wits with an antagonist that has a personality and presence, almost as if the hunter were dealing with a human adversary.

The stories of Jim Corbett, are therefore a kind of Bible for all those who set out on the perilous sport of man eater hunting. Unfortunately stories about man eating wolves are scanty. The wolf as an animal has been the subject of many myths and legends but there is a dearth of scientific data, about its habits in the wild. For some reason, which I find difficult to fathom, the wolf is considered a close kin of man. There are stories of men transforming themselves, into wolves or *werewolves* and praying upon other men, and these are current in all cultural traditions. In popular lore therefore the wolf is invariably an evil animal, usually with supernatural powers. This explains, why, whenever there are cases of man eating wolves, people so readily believe tales of sorcery and witchcraft and quite often some unfortunate individual on whom suspicion falls, is lynched for being a witch or evil spirit.

On the other hand, there are many stories of human children being brought up by wolves and behaving for all practical purposes like a wolf in human form. Some of those stories are by authors of undoubted integrity, whose veracity one can not doubt. These stories of wolves, suckling and nursing human children, bring out the same aspect of their character, namely their closeness to human beings. Curiously, it is this almost human aspect of wolves which has given them the reputation of being embodiments of evil.

At the same time stories of man eating wolves have not been well documented. In fact, when we were faced with this menace, we did not know of any. It is natural therefore to assume that the man eater, when rarely one comes across such an animal, must be a single animal. There is also the obvious fascination of dealing with a single animal, of fabulous size and cunning ;given the reputation of wolves, such a supposition seems natural. The story of a gigantic beast, driven to killing human beings by the impulse of innate evil makes a rattling good yarn, it is much more interesting than the reality of a whole pack of mangy, underfed animals, driven to the desperate expedient of killing humans, because of the destruction of their natural habitat and prey. For all these reasons, we started the whole operation with the assumption that we were dealing with a single animal, and we continued to believe in this theory, until we had to abandon it when the killings continued even after Shahjade had killed the big wolf. It would be fair to say that this mistake cost the district a few more lives, though it is hard to see what alternative course of action we could have followed. Now with the wisdom of hindsight, let me say that, it is a fair assumption, when ever one comes across a man eating wolf, that one is dealing with, not one single animal, but a whole pack.

Our second mistake was to have followed a strategy of static defence. By static defence I mean the policy of posting sharpshooters at selected locations, in the hope that the wolf might be caught unawares, while following its normal routes. On the face of it, this was a sound policy. We had put up marksmen at places which were frequented by the wolf, and there was every reason to believe that sooner or later the wolf or wolves would fall into the ambush. It was reasonable to suppose that the man eater would eventually turn up at one of the water holes or commonly used game trails, where our men were lying in wait for it, day and night. Again with the benefit of hindsight, it can be said, that this is unlikely to happen. The wolf is an extremely wary animal and it would not just walk into an ambush. Something more is needed to complete a successful trap when dealing with wolves, the trap has to be so baited that the wolf is induced to take the bait, this calls for a lot of ingenuity and planning, but it can be done. But in any case, the policy of simply waiting for the wolf to make a mistake is something that is bound to fail. In retrospect, what is needed is either a policy of hot pursuit, or of baiting the trap in such a way that the wolf is made to overcome its normal instinct for caution and take the bait. The policy of hot pursuit, yielded results when the wolf was tracked down to its lair and ambushed by the Pardhis. It was more or less the same policy that was followed by Shahjade when he pursued the wolf, and shot it when it was still at the kill. It was providential that he happened to on the spot when the wolf killed the lamb, for had he been even a few minutes late, I feel sure the wolf would have got away.

The question that arises naturally is, what kind of bait will entice the wolf. Our experience shows that here again the conventional method of tying up a bait at a waterhole or some other location and waiting for the wolf to take it, will not work. Considering the suspicious nature of wolves, it is unlikely that it will accept a bait that is offered to it on a platter, as it were. It was our experience that time and again, the wolf walked away from the bait, after having virtually walked up to it. To circumvent the customary wariness of the wolf it is necessary that the bait should be offered is such a manner that it does not look like a bait at all. The Shahjade incident shows how this can be done. If for instance a hunter dressed up as a shepherd, follows a herd of sheep or goats, the suspicions of the wolf shall not be aroused. What could be more natural than a shepherd leading his flock, over choice grazing fields. Who would suspect that one of the shepherds is not a shepherd but a hunter. As we saw in the Shahjade case such a ruse is likely to work.

Wolves prefer young lambs and goat kids and are likely to accept the bait when it is offered in the manner described above. There is also the possibility of using human decoys, which we unsuccessfully tried out, during the bullock cart ride. That mission did not succeed, because the wolf, chose another victim, but it did lull its suspicions and made it come out in the open. A rather more successful incident of using a human decoy, or rather making the wolf believe that we were using a human bait, will be described presently. The point remains that using conventional method of tying up baits, or sitting up over likely spots is not going to yield results and we were being naïve when we thought that such methods might work.

Finally, I think it might have been useful if we had told the people of the area exactly what to expect, and the kind of animal we were dealing with. This could have been done by printing pamphlets, and other literature detailing the appearance, and habits of wolves and the precautions that they might take to avoid being attacked. This would have nipped the rumours in the bud and checked panic. I commend these methods to all those who have to deal with such a menace in future.

A farewell party

It so happened that Kaurav, who had played a stellar role in organizing the logistical side of our operations was now transferred out of Ashta. His place was to be taken by Sharma, a tall genial man with a bluff manner, who was well connected politically. I was sorry to see Kaurav go, but these things happen and there was nothing that could be done about it. As is usual on these occasions, a party was organised to bid farewell to the outgoing officer. Such parties are a routine occurrence in official life, but they still provide an insight into the working of the small town milieu in which district officers have to spend their working life.

This party was held in the Tehsil premises at Ashta. This building, as I have mentioned elsewhere, was situated atop the local fort. This fort was built on a small knoll on the left bank of the Parvati River. The walls and fortifications of this fort had crumbled away, but the main doorway still stood. This was a huge arched gateway, surmounted by two small cupolas, the whole still being in a state of surprisingly good repair. A steep cobbled pathway led up to the Tehsil building, which must have housed the local garrison as well in state times, but now was too dilapidated even to be used as an office. Some land near the Indore highway had already been earmarked for the new Tehsil, but its construction was going to take quite a few years, and in the meantime the old building despite its ruinous state continued to be the administrative centre of the Tehsil. This building had a large courtyard within its portals, and this was where the party was held.

I had been touring in Ashta, looking for the wolf, and on the day of the party I called an early halt to the proceedings and headed straight for the tehsil premises. The party was scheduled to be held at five in the evening. Making allowances for the lackadaisical habits of the locals I had arrived on the spot at ten past five but when I reached the tehsil building I found that except for Kaurav and his subordinates, none of the guests had turned up. This was not entirely unexpected, but I still decided to take my allotted seat in the middle of a large semicircle of chairs. I reasoned that if the guests found me absent, the party may be further delayed, while if they found me already present, their embarrassment may induce them to shed their usual dilatory methods.

The seating arrangements on this occasion may be of some interest, as they throw some light on the manner in which the official hierarchy is organized in a small town. To my right sat Kaurav and to his right, Sharma, the new incumbent. The chair to my left was vacant, but not for long. Som dutt the local correspondent of a Bhopal based newpaper, one of the first guests to arrive, occupied the chair. The other guests now began to arrive in ones and twos. The guests included a fair sprinkling of lawyers, and local politicians as well as few journalists.

I noticed that there was an unwritten order of precedence among these guests in the matter of seating and each person was careful to follow it. Next to Kaurav and Sharma, sat the other administrative officers posted at the Tehsil level including the local Circle Inspector of Police C.P. Singh, who was also know as Raja Sahib due to his supposedly royal lineage. Next to the officers was the solid phalanx of lawyers, all clad in their dark jackets, with some even sporting the white judicial collar. To my right were the politicians, first the local MLA, then the Janpad members and then the rural Sarpanchas, or headmen, who were to be distinguished from the more urbanised politicians by their distinctive attire. Most of these rural grandees wore a saffron or yellow turban over white Kurta and dhoti, while many wore black tunics as well as Kurtas.

Som Dutt the journalist who sat next to me had thus violated the pecking order that seemed to be in force, but as members of the press are allowed a wide latitude in all matters of protocol, others, though resentful, were helpless.

Som Dutt did nothing to mitigate this resentment. He was in fact enjoying the flutter that he was causing, and to make sure that people took note of his presumptive status, he often lent towards me to whisper the most inconsequential things in a most conspiratorial manner. First he said,"Sir! You must be tired after your journey."

Nonsense! Som Dutt, as you know I have been camping in Ashta.

"Then he said," Sir!, do you know why these Sarpanchas are wearing saffron turbans?"

"No, I can't imgaine why?"

"Sir! they are declaring their political affiliation. As you know saffron is a colour that is used by a particular political party. "

"But I thought this was the customary headgear in this area."

"That is true sir, but the normal turban is lemon yellow rather than saffron, as you, may have noticed."

Now that he mentioned it, I could see he had a point. However before I could I reply the person who sat to the right of leant right across him and whispered to me, "Sir!, I want five minutes from you after this function. I want to discuss something important with you."

"What is Shivnarain ji! if it is important certainly, you can see me when we go in for the refreshments."

"Sir, it is about the activities of our local forest guard, I shall tell you all about it when we talk."

Shivnarain Malviya was the local member of the Legislative Assembly. This was his fourth term as MLA, but he had never been considered for ministerial office. This was not difficult to understand, because he was barely educated, and quite indifferent to the attractions of office. He was loved rather for his phlegmatic nature, his honesty, and his accessibility. It was out of character for him to lean across and speak to me at a function, but I could see that he was irritated with Som Dutt for having occupied the chair that belonged by right to him. Som Dutt's constant whispering had added insult to injury. It was to avenge himself for this imagined slight that he had leant across Som Dutt.

But just then the Master of Ceremonies, the local tehsiladar, Mr Tiwari, a short portly man whose dignity bordered on pomposity took the mike to begin the proceedings. After a brief and flowery welcome address, he asked for the assembled guests to come up one by one and garland the chief guest. The tehsildar called out the names of the guests in an order of precedence and they all came up to the guest of honour, Kaurav and put a garland round his neck. After a while some of the more enterprising guests took two garlands from the peon who stood with garlands hanging around a short stick, and put a garland around the neck of the new incumbent as well. Some of them even made a move towards me, but I waved them away towards Kaurav. By the time the tehsildar came to the end of the guest lists, I thought Sharma had been more profusely garlanded than Kaurav. It was an obvious, but rather crude illustration of the old adage that every one salutes the rising sun.

After the garlanding it was time for valedictory speeches and the first person who was called upon to say a few words was, Mr Quereshi, the president of the local bar council. Quereshi was an elderly gentleman with a thick mop of grizzled hair, a dark complexion and an aggressive and voluble manner. He cleared his throat importantly and began –

"Mr. Kaurav, our outgoing SDM, honourable Collector Sahib, Mr Sharma our new SDM, respected MLA sahib, janab Shivnarain ji, tehsildar sahib ..."

Mr Qureshi was careful to include everyone in his address whom he considered of sufficient importance. His long litany finally ended with, "and all those honourable guests whom I have not mentioned by name, but who have graced this occasion with their presence. As you all know we are gathered here to bid good bye to our Mr Kaurav, who has served the people of this tehsil with unremitting devotion for three long years. I have seen many officers in my long years as a member of the bar, but I have seldom seen an officer so hardworking, so affable, so assiduous in redressing the wrongs of the people. We shall indeed miss his ever cheerful countenance and presence but, I am sure he shall be a boon to the people wherever he goes.

I would also like, on this occasion to welcome Mr Sharma, who is going to succeed Mr Kaurav. We have great expectations from Mr Sharma. I am sure he will carry on the good work of his predecessor. Indeed, we expect him to set new and even higher standards of excellence, if this were possible. Before I conclude I must highlight a local issue of grave importance, because our Collector Sahib is here, and I am sure he will take appropriate action in the matter. This is the question of maintaining law and order on Holi, which this year is going to fall on a Friday. People will be returning from their Friday Namaz at the same time, as the Holi revellers will be coming back. It is important to ensure that miscreants do not take any advantage of the situation. We have to ensure that the communal harmony which has always been the pride of our town is maintained.

I also want to put forward another small problem before the Collector Sahib. It is good that our respected MLA is also here. This is the problem of the tehsil building. As you can all see, this building is in a most dangerous state and any untoward incident can happen any time, leading to avoidable loss of life. We lawyers feel apprehensive, at pleading our cases in such a dilapidated court house. It detracts from the majesty of law and the dignity of justice. There is also the danger that if raise our voice, the roof may come crashing down."

He paused to see if there was any reaction to this attempt at levity, but no one laughed. Mr Quereshi went on,"There are many other problems that deserve mention but I will not try your patience now by mentioning them. But before I conclude let me say a few words about the wolf menace that has afflicted our tehsil for the last two months and the role played by the administration in combating it. We are deeply grateful to our Collector, for having spared no pains to bring these animals to book, and we hope the remaining man eaters shall soon be accounted for. Once again I give my best wishes to Mr Kaurav and welcome Mr Sharma. Thank you, gentlemen, for giving me such a patient hearing."

After Mr Quereshi it was the turn of the MLA, who should have actually been the first to speak, had he not for some reason left his seat and gone out for a while. Just as he got back, the tehsildar, called upon him to take the mike. He delivered the following peroration in his own bumbling way.

"Honourable, Collector Sahib, Mr Kaurav, Mr...er Sharma, and friends, you know I am a plain spoken man and not very adept at giving fine speeches. All I can say is, all I can say is ..." there was a long and embarrassing pause at this juncture and then after taking off and putting on his white Gandhi cap, he resumed," all I can say is that Mr Kaurav was a good officer, a very good officer and I hope his successor will also be a good officer. We have a lot of poor people in this tehsil and we need officers with a human touch. This brings me to another subject which I wanted to mention – and that is the subject of the man eating wolf. I want the government to give some compensation to the families of the victims. I know nothing will recompense these families for the loss which they have suffered, but at least we can come to their aid in this time of trouble by lending them a helping hand. I hope the Collector, who is himself a very humane person, will make some announcement today in this regard. Thank you."

The other speakers, rambled on in the same vein, but all of them took care to demand compensation, once the matter had been raised by the MLA, and each wanted to outdo the other in suggesting how much compensation should be paid. At the end of it all I was asked to say a few words in conclusion. If memory serves me right, this is what I said," Mr Kaurav, Mr Sharma, Shivnarainji and friends, all of you have spoken of the many good qualities of Kaurav and I want to add my own support to everything that you have said. Mr Kaurav, who is leaving us to take up another assignment in a neighbouring district has done a commendable job in Ashta Tehsil. In particular I want to place on record the signal service that he has rendered the people of this tehsil in organizing the logistical side of our operations against the man eating wolf of Ashta. He has been to all the affected villages, toured the area day and night, and in everything has been a tower of strength to me and indeed to the entire administration. (Shouts of hear, hear, and some clapping.)We shall certainly miss his services, but then I am sure where ever he is posted, he will always be an asset to the government.

I would also like to welcome his successor, Mr Sharma, who is an able an experienced officer and will I am sure, give a good account of himself in his new charge. Thank You."

But as I handed over the mike to the tehsildar to conclude the ceremony there were shouts from several quarters that I had not said anything about the issue of compensation. So I had to again take the mike," Friends, I appreciate your concern about the bereaved families, I share this concern and will do everything in my power to mitigate their suffering, including the payment of compensation. But you will appreciate the fact that a final decision in the matter can only be taken by the state government. I will recommend to them that compensation should be paid on as generous a scale as possible, but I will urge you once again, not to make political capital out of a tragic situation. I seek your co-operation in destroying the remaining wolves – so that our people can once again lead their lives, free from the spectre of fear. If God wills, we shall soon succeed in our objective."

This met with a rousing reception. Thereafter the tehsildar stood to say the last words. But he was as long winded and diffuse as the rest of the speakers. He went on at great length about the great wisdom and capabilities of Kaurav. Having done with Kaurav, he launched into a panegyric about what a wonderful man Sharma was. It seemed the whole world could hardly boast of two such paragons as Sharma and Kaurav. As the tehsildar showed no inclination to end his speech, many of the guests got up to leave and some made for the adjoining marquee where the eatables were laid out. The tesildar took the hint and wound up his grandiloquent oration with a final flourish and a 'Jai Hind' after which everyone rushed post haste towards the refreshments, forgetting protocol. When we reached the tent, they were tucking into the food with gusto. Thus ended the farewell party and the curtain was brought down on the role of Kaurav in the whole drama.

How the compensation was sanctioned

The story of how the government was finally induced to sanction compensation, is not without its funny side and must be told. Immediately after this farewell party, I prepared a proposal for compensation to be given to the parents of all those killed by the wolf and sent it to the state government, assuming that the matter will be approved in due course, within a week or two. This was naïve optimism. As a civil servant, who had put in almost ten years of service, I should have known better. Anything, which is applied for, petitioned or demanded, is never sanctioned in due course by the government. The first instinct of the Leviathan is to ignore any attempt to seek its intercession, if this inertia is surmounted and its attention is somehow captured its instinct is to say no. The only time when the government can be persuaded to put aside its instinct to say no, is when the initiative comes from on high ;from the political leadership. Whenever ordinary mortals are involved, the desired result can only be achieved after a great deal of effort.

I should not have been surprised therefore, when Ganeshan, who was then Deputy Secretary in the Forest Department, told me, in response to my queries, that he could not trace the file containing my proposal, if indeed such a proposal existed in the first place. He felt that trying to locate the file would be a futile exercise, it would resurface in its own time, in accordance with a mysterious law whose workings could not be predicted, and in the meantime the best course open to me, was to submit a fresh proposal, and if I was really anxious to save time, to bring the papers personally and get them processed. This I did.

But when I took the matter up to the Forest Secretary, a man by the name of Shivendra, he told me that his department had no scheme for giving compensation to parents of children killed by wolves. He did have a provision for people killed by tigers, or for people mauled by tigers or leopards. There was also a scheme for compensating owners of cattle lifted by tigers and leopards. But wolves! no one had ever thought that such a contingency would ever arise and consequently his departmental budget had no provision for it. Shivendra was a stickler for procedures, and he maintained that there was a generic difference between wolves and tigers, in other words the existing budget provisions could not accommodate this contingency and therefore the matter would have to be sent to the Finance Department for their approval. To the FD thus I went.

The Finance Department has a quiver full of arrows for dealing with proposals for expenditure. They seldom believe in outright refusal. Their favourite tactic is to return the proposal to the concerned departments with a set of queries, which are calculated to delay the matter. If these queries are answered by some chance, they are followed by another set of questions, entirely unrelated to the first set. When the proposer is completely frustrated by this inquisition, the matter is finally dismissed with some pregnant remark, like 'the matter is not in the public interest', or 'the proposal should be included in the next year's budget.'

Another standard device is to refer the matter to some other nodal department. The state government has several such departments. For instance the Law Department is handy for examining the legal implications of any proposal and thus delaying the matter indefinitely. The General Administration Department is available, for supplying the GAD angle, which means examining the matter in the light of past practice and precedent. As their is a precedent to support or reject anything, this practice only serves to delay the matter. Finally there is also the Planning Department, where many promising ideas meet with an untimely end, even before they can be said to be born in the official sense. It was to the Planning Department that the FD had decided to refer my proposal.

The Planning Secretary at that time was Shekhawat who was a rare man, in the sense that, alone among the cynical self seeking tribe of senior civil servants, he took himself and his job with a fanatical seriousness. Shekhawat was a man of rare honour, of complete integrity, of almost boring transparency, but for all his well intentioned industry, he was completely ineffective, because Planning is the last thing that is taken seriously in the government and the only way to make sense of the job of being the Planning Secretary is to leave the matter of Planning to clerks and to let chaos reign.

Shekhawat was a tall, martial looking figure, with a booming parade ground voice, in which he was fond of holding forth to those who went to see him on official business, in the manner of a Professor lecturing to a rather dull class of students. He was full of theoretical formulations about everything under the sun and had a genius for putting across simple things in elegantly obscure phraseology. When I went to see him, he was, as usual smoking, this being the only liberty that he permitted himself to take with official decorum.

"Ah, Ajay! what brings you to the Planning Department? Have a cigarette." Shekhawat affected a fraternal interest in the affairs of his juniors. He still believed that the civil service was a fraternity and though he would harangue everyone black and blue, he would never forget to order tea and biscuits for you and treat you with old fashioned curtsey.

"It is about this wolf menace sir! I have proposed that compensation should be paid to the parents of those killed by the wolf, but the finance department thinks the matter should be first sent to the Planning Department."

"Well, as this year's Plan has already been approved by the Planning Commission, and the budget is before the Vidhan Sabha, I don't see what we can do at this stage. In any case proposals of this kind do not fall within the purview of the Planning Department. Surely the Forest Department have a scheme for cases of this kind."

"Well they do and they don't. They do have a scheme for victims of tigers and leopards, but none for wolf victims. Simply because such a thing has never occurred before."

"I see! in that case your case should go to the Finance Department. The Planning Department deals with what can be foreseen and planned for. The unforeseen falls within the Finance Department's ambit – they have something call the 'contingency fund', for just such cases."

"Thanks, sir, for enlightening me. By the way, before I leave, tell me one more thing, will this come within Plan or Non-Plan."

"Oh! Non-Plan definitely, anything that has to be done, like the payment of salaries and pensions, comes within Non-Plan. The Plan is only a statement of intent. It deals with what ought to be done, but sadly, seldom gets done."

This was the distilled wisdom of years. Shekhawat was being

unusually frank and had put aside his didactic manner to tell me these home truths. We shared a companionable smoke and I took my case back to the Finance Department with the backing of the Planning Secretary.

The Finance Secretary in those days was Shivlingam. One of those clever, competent officers, who also have the happy knack of getting along with politicians and superiors. I took the matter to him pleading that the compensation be sanctioned from the contingency fund.

Shivalingam looked at me speculatively as if surprised at my ignorance, yet not knowing how to respond. Finally he said, "Yadav, its clear you have no notion of how the Finance Deprtment works. You ought to have known that the contingency fund is all but exhausted, and we still have more than three months of the Financial Year still to go. What will I do if a real contingency turns up."

I argued that the sudden appearance of the man eating wolf and its impact on the lives of the people of Ashta Tehsil, was a real contingency. But Shivalingam laughed. "No, no, I mean a real contingency, in fact such a contingency is imminent. There is going to be a massive cabinet expansion next month and all the ministers would want brand new cars. Now where will I get the money for it except from the contingency fund. You understand, don't you, that ministers looking for new cars is a real contingency and no Finance Secretary could turn down such a proposal."

I had not realised, until then, that the Finance Department's scale of priorities was quite different from mine. Now I did.

"But sir, in that case, what happens to my proposal?", I asked.

"Your proposal, young man, forms a new item of expenditure, and the matter can not be approved even by the cabinet. If we play by the rules, there is no option but to put in the matter in the next years budget and present it to the Vidhan Sabha."

"But sir! I can't wait until then. You will, I am sure appreciate my predicament. I have to do something for the people of my district."

"Yes, yes, but the Finance Department exists to tell people what can't be done." He looked at me with a bored look, then picked up another file from the small pile that lay on his table with a languid grace, signifying that the interview was over.

This encounter with the FD put me in a bad humour. I was walking down the corridor that leads out of the secretariat building, when I ran into Harinder Singh alias Old Harry. Harry was what you call an old hand, he had been around for years and years. He had already reached the top of the profession, he was Additional Chief Secretary, nominally on par with the Chief Secretary. He was a maverick and had several interesting and sensible maxims about administration. One of his maxims was – any man who stays in office after office hours is a fool. He also maintained that a man's competence was in inverse proportion to the time he spent in office. In appearance he was a tall, lumbering man with a shock of white hair. Harry stood in *loco parentis* to all the young officers who were not fired with a zeal for self advancement and had some sympathy for his outlook on life. I certainly looked up to him, and he was consequently more than usually indulgent to me. When he saw me, walking off with my head down, he guessed that all was not well.

"Well, young man, why should you look so glum. Come on, have a cup of tea with me, and tell me what has put you in this frame of mind."

"Sir, I have just been to see the Finance Secretary."

"Ah! that explains everything. Say no more. Hey! Ramsingh, get us some tea, will you, and make sure its good *karak* tea, and not the ditchwater that serve in this building."

Ramsingh busied himself in boiling water in a kettle that stood in one corner of his room. Harry in the meanwhile began again, "I know how you feel. This Shivalingam is a bloody constipated prig. One would have thought, with a name like that he would have a little more spunk in him, but no, the fellow has no balls. Thinks he is a bloody mandarin!but you should see him before the CM. Ajay, have you seen a man shrink, I mean literally shrink with sycophancy, fold in his arms, draw in his limbs and generally reduce himself to the stature of a wriggling worm, if you haven't then you should see the way Shivalingam stands before the Chief Minister. Ha, ha."

Harry laughed at the recollection of Shivalingam before the CM. I thought to myself, that Harry's description could fit not only the Finance Secretary, but a host of other senior civil servants, and unaccountably I recalled the lines of poem by John Betjeman, which talk about the brains of a senior civil servant being 'sweetbread on the road today.' I was in that kind of a mood. But over a strong cup of properly brewed tea, Harry was able to get the whole story out of me and I felt better, for having found a sympathetic listener.

After having heard my story Harry laughed again."Is that all, well I'll tell you what you should do. Go ahead and sanction the compensation and draw the money. As Collector you have the power to take such action in emergencies. After you have done what you think proper, send a SOS to the CM stressing the negative consequences that would have followed, if you had not acted in anticipation of sanction. If my judgement is right, you will not only get your compensation sanctioned, but also a letter of commendation from the government."

As things turned out Harry was proved to be a better prophet than others, and events happened exactly as he had predicted. Not only was the compensation sanctioned *ex post facto* by the government, but I also received a letter of commendation from the CM for having shown exemplary presence of mind and devotion to duty in this matter.

Strange happening in Dodi Rest House

I have told you in passing about the strange things that were supposed to happen in Dodi Rest House. Despite its nondescript appearance, this old building has, or at least one of the rooms in the building had, a rather sinister aura. This is the bed room that is away from the road. On the face of it, there is nothing remarkable about this room. It is as commonplace as the Rest House itself. It flanks the large hall, which serves as a drawing as well as dining room. This hall has a high ceiling, and the dim light when the ventilators and windows are shut down in summer can make the room appear quite cavernous and spooky. But nothing out of the ordinary has ever been reported to have happened in this room. There is a real fireplace on one side, the old furniture there has a certain character, and it can be conceded that the room has a certain old world charm.

But the same thing can't be said about the room next door. This is a drab, twelve by twelve room, with a much lower ceiling, which slopes down towards the outer wall. The room has a wooden bedstead, a small cupboard in one corner, and a chair and writing table that are almost of regulation size and appearance. There is a tiny bathroom attached to the bedroom. No one looking at this room can imagine that it can have any connection with the supernatural, but as any of the locals, specially the older men will tell you, spending a night in the room can sometimes lead to unexpected events.

Naturally there is a story attached to this room. The story concerns a Sahib, who was probably, the senior engineer in the Public Works Department of the Bhopal state. This sahib was also a shikari and whenever he came down to Dodi on official work, he brought his guns with him, to take advantage of the plentiful game that was to be found in the vicinity of Dodi. In those far off days. Shikar, was in fact the favoured pastime of the nobility of Bhopal, and the sahib's love of shikar was looked upon with indulgent regard by the Nawab and his court. He was after all only engaged in what they also considered the only sport deserving of a man's consideration.

Well, it was a winter day that promised a fair day's shooting, and the Sahib had spent the whole day chasing a bear in the jungles around Rampur, a few miles south of Dodi. Bears are easy game, especially when they are out grubbing for roots or termites. When a bear has put down his snout into a termite hill to suck them out, he will hardly deign to notice any shikari who has the temerity to stalk him at these moments. This particular bear however had an annoying habit of wandering off just when the sahib got within shooting distance. The sahib however lacked nothing in persistence, he followed the bear up and down innumerable ravines which were overgrown with lantana bushes, and which left him bruised and bleeding. After a few hours of this fruitless effort, he gave up. When he got back to the Dodi Rest House, footsore and weary, with thorns and thistles sticking into his stockings, night was setting in.

It was the Sahib's practice, like the rest of his compatriots in India, to start the evening with a few sundowners. A table was thus laid out for him on the lawns of the Rest House, where it was a little cooler than the stuffy air within the Dak bungalow. It was a dark night, with a slight breeze and isolated clouds scudding across the sky. Quite pleasant really, with the stars coming out and the heat of the day dissipating gradually. But the Sahib was not content to sip his drink and enjoy the evening. He was still thinking of the bear. He did not enjoy missing his prey, and this bear had come so maddeningly close and yet eluded him. He kept playing out the events of the day in his mind's eye and reviewing his mistakes. It was easy, sitting in an armchair, with a tall drink in his hand, to outwit the bear every time. So busy was he in this make believe hunt that he hardly realized how much he had drunk He was through with his sixth large drink, when he asked the Khansama to serve dinner, and also to bring him his gun.

Dinner, even in an upcountry Rest House was a ceremonious affair in those days. The dishes were brought out under starched coverlets, in silver or at least pewter containers. I don't know what the khansama had dished out that day. It might have been mulligatawny soup followed by curried chicken and rounded off by plum pudding, I don't know. All I know is, that it was when he decided to wash down his dinner with another large rum, that he finally shot his bolt, and when the khansama came out to clear the table, he took him for the bear and shot him dead in his tracks.

It was this khansamah who haunted the Rest House. He was seen sometimes as a dark spectral presence wandering about the compound. Strangers staying at the bungalow, who didn't know about this ghostly presence often took him to be one of the staff, and there are amusing stories of visitors calling him up, only to find after a while that what they had taken to be a man was only a wavering shadow and that they were yelling into thin air. There were also those who said that they often heard unaccountable knockings in the night and the sound of some one walking about. No one had however been harmed.

It seemed this was a benign ghost.

Before I recount what happened one night when I was sojourning there, let me tell you how I came to be spending the night in the Rest House in the first place. It was the night of Diwali, the festival of light, which every Hindu likes to celebrate with family and friends. Diwali is a big day for children, one to which they look forward for weeks. Firecrackers and sparklers are stockpiled in advance and thousand of *diyas* or earthen lamps are lit to usher in the festival of light. Diwali is also a good time for those who love sweets, as I do. My wife takes care to prepare all my favourite sweets for Diwali, even if she is not so obliging the rest of the year.

Well the usual festive mood that year was dampened by the wolf menace, but the Diwali spirit can't be completely dashed. My children had collected their usual assortment of firecrackers, and swirlers and sparklers and rockets and were creating a merry din, when I received a phone call from Ashta that a child had been killed close to the Dodi Rest House by the wolf. There was nothing for it but to say good bye to the children and set off for Dodi.

About two furlongs from the Rest House, close to the foot of the Dodi ghati is a power sub station. A child, who lived in the nearby village of Dodi had wandered out in the evening, thinking that it would be quite safe as the sub station was virtually next to the highway. There used to be a small tea shop there, and perhaps the child wanted to have a glass of tea, but the shop happened to be closed on account of Diwali. It is possible that finding the shop closed the boy sat down to watch the traffic, as boys do sometimes. In any case, the wolf pounced on him as he was sitting by the roadside. He had time to cry out once, and his despairing cry was heard by a passer by, who sounded the alarm. The villagers were able to send forth a search party within minutes, and they soon found the boy. Frightened by all the noise that they were making, the wolf had made off in the nick of time, but the boy was quite dead. The wolf had sunk his fangs deep in his throat, and his life had ebbed out. All I could do after reaching the spot was to console the parents.

As I had no heart left for Diwali celebrations after this unfortunate incident, I decided to spend the night in Dodi. I had never before slept in the Rest House and was unaware of its ghost. But it was a melancholy night that I prepared to pass in the Dak Bungalow. It was a bad enough to be parted from one's family on Diwali night, it was much worse to be spending the night in a dinghy old room, alone and without cheerful company or cheering news.

As it happened I was lodged in the far bed room. The other bed room was occupied by a PWD engineer, and although my staff was insistent that I get the room vacated, I thought it unnecessary to put the sub engineer to so much bother, for the sake of just one night. This bed room I have already described briefly above. It was a small room, with a sloping roof. The room had three doors, one of which led to the veranada outside, the second to the drawing room which was adjacent, and the third to the attached bathroom. It had only one large window with an iron grill across it. This window, which was a large wooden affair painted a dark green, as PWD windows and doors sometimes are, opened inwards, so that it could only be opened by some one within the room. It could not be opened from the outside, because of the iron grill. The only remarkable thing in the room was a rather fine print of a tiger killing a black buck, in a jungle. This print, somehow had a faintly sinister aspect to it. It showed a ruined house in one corner, with a small clearing in front, which was fringed by thick jungle. It was in this clearing that the tiger standing up on his hind legs, was shown killing the deer, down whose flanks, a trickle of blood was flowing. There was a hint of a shadowy presence, looking out from one of the windows of the ruined house, though it was hard to pin point whether it was really a human figure, or something else. The most dramatic thing in the scenery was the sky, a heavy, black, lowering sort of sky, which seemed to be the presage of a tremendous storm. And in fact a bolt of lightening was shown flashing from one of the clouds.

It was a cold and windy night, so I remember I had shut the window, but probably did not bolt it. The rain had warped the old wooden frame of the window and when it was shut, the bolt was slightly out of alignment and it was not so easy to fasten it, without a great deal of wrenching and pulling. But the heavy timber and the warp meant that the window did not move smoothly on its hinges and no gust of wind would be able to open it. Some of these thoughts probably passed through my mind as I shut the window, put out the light and went to sleep.

I don't know how long I slept, but at some point in the night I found my self wide awake. The stiff breeze that had been blowing earlier had died down and it was deathly quiet. In the sepulchral silence I heard, or thought I heard a gentle scratching and knocking at the window. As I have mentioned the window had a grill and a wire mesh across it, which made it impossible for some one standing outside to open it. Yet this is what, if my senses did not mislead me, I was now witnessing. For one of the halves of the window now swung open, as though pushed by some one from the outside. As I have already said, the window was virtually jammed on its frame, and it could not swing open in this noiseless fashion, like the swing doors of a saloon, yet this is what had happened. I had a sense that someone was peeping in through the opening, though I could see nothing when I stood up to peer out. However the sense of being under surveillance persisted. I was unsettled by what I had seen, but I had to investigate this business further. I had my. 12 bore gun with me, this I picked up and was outside in a flash. I had no kind of light with me and it was still quite dark, but again I sensed rather than saw a presence, a dark insubstantial figure that seemed to melt into the darkness as I yelled, *Kaun hai* – who is there? – knowing that no one would respond to my query. But here I was again wrong, some where far away in the depths of the night, a wolf called suddenly, as if responding to my shouted challenge. The eerie sound rose in volume and intensity, rising and falling like passing gusts of wind on a stormy night, before dying away. Then the silence and the darkness closed in again, leaving me alone with the mystery. To this day I have no satisfactory explanation for the manner in which the window had opened. It must have been the resident ghost playing one of his usual pranks on me, or may be my senses were overwrought, and I had imagined the whole thing. I will leave the whole thing to the judgement of the reader and get on with my story.

Achhan Mian's orchard

As one climbs the Dodi plateau from the Ashta side, the large village of Khadi is seen a few miles to the north. The village is clearly visible in the distance as a collection of whitewashed dwellings. It can be identified easily by the immensely tall microwave tower that stands guarding the entrance to the village. If one continues to follow the track further north, beyond the village of Khadi, one comes across Achhan Mian's orchard. This orchard, which must be at least fifty acres in extent, produces the best mango in the district. It has also a good number of guava and orange trees, but the mango trees are its glory. These are stalwart trees, many of them sixty or even seventy years old, and they stand in regular rows and columns, like the massed ranks of some gigantic arboreal army. Each tree is veritable giant, a real "green robed senator of the woods", and the dark green umbrage of these trees creates an ocean of shade that is cool and pleasant even in the hottest summer.

I have said nothing about the mango fruit that is produced by these trees, because to tell the truth I like fruits which have a tang and pungency in them and find the mango too tame for my taste. But those who are partial to the fruit, swear by Achhan Mian's mangoes. The owner of this green pleasance is himself quite a remarkable personage. Achhan Mian today is a venerable old man. No one knows his exact age, apart from himself, but he couldn't be less than eighty now, if he is a day. But even now he is upright and hale and walks about, without the aid of a stick. The only concession that he has made to age is that he has given up dyeing his beard with henna, so that it now flows over his chest, as white as snow. In those days however, he used to dye his beard and clip it short, so that with his fair colour and neat red beard, he looked almost like a Turk.

Achhan Mian had a house in Sehore, and this establishment was presided over by his younger wife. Whenever he came to Sehore, which was quite often, he made it point to seek an appointment with me. He was one of the few visitors I had, who never had any official work with me and came merely to exchange pleasantries. When ever he visited me, Achhan Mian wore a ceremonial dress, which in his case was a sherwani and a fez. His sherwani was always immaculate, his fez appeared just that shade of red which is found only in a newly brushed and carefully tended fez and it had a beautiful silken tassel which was further testimony of the care he lavished on the cap. It was obvious that Achhan Mian set great store by ceremony. When ever he met me, he would produce, with great deliberation, an engraved silver box in which he kept his *paan.* Although Achhan Mian knew, I did not eat *paan,* it did not stop him from producing his silver box with a flourish and offering me its contents. After I had politely declined, the box would be replaced, and honour satisfied, we would get around to talking of other things. He never failed to invite me to his orchard, and truth to tell, I never failed to avail of his offer whenever opportunity arose, because there was no better place for a *siesta* on a hot summer afternoon, in the entire district

When Achhan Mian met me after the appearance of the wolf in his neck of the woods, he looked obviously a worried man. "Huzoor", he began straight away, "I have something serious to tell you."

"What is it Achhan Mian, has your favourite dog fallen ill?"

"No, huzoor."

"Then has some disease affected the mango trees?"

"No, huzoor, it is about the wolf."

"The wolf, well what about it, has the wolf suddenly developed a fondness for mangoes.?"

I regretted my ill timed joke the moment I cracked it. The old gentlemen had a pained look on his face, but was too well bred to make any protest.

"No huzoor, I have seen two wolves moving about the orchard a number of times, and thought I must tell you about it. You know I keep a herd of goats at the orchard. I suspect the wolves are attracted by these animals – and not – I think by the mangoes ", he said with a twinkle in his eyes.

I realized that the matter was serious and presented an opportunity that must be taken. I knew Achhan Mian was a good shikari so I asked him what he had done to get a shot at the wolves.

"Well huzoor! I have sat up a number of times, sometimes spending the entire night in a fruitless vigil, but the accursed animals never turn up whenever I am sitting up. It is as if they have a sixth sense which warns them of the danger that awaits them. They are seen only when everyone is off guard and disappear by the time one can get hold of a rifle. I am beginning to believe this non sense put out by the villagers that we are dealing not with a mere animal but with an evil spirit."

"Nonsense Achhan Mian! I have a plan which I would like to put into action if it meets with your approval."

I outlined my proposal to Achhan Mian, he approved naturally, and in consequence the next afternoon found me at the orchard. My plan was based on the experience that we had gathered so far, especially the experience of Shahjade, which led me to believe that one could not just passively wait for the wolf to turn up. Some more active inducement as well as deception had to be tried out. My plan was to dress up as a shepherd and spend my nights with the goats in their *kraal* – never mind the smell – in the hope that the wolf would sooner or later turn up and unsuspecting, fall into my trap.

When I got to the orchard, the sun was still high in the heavens, and it was still hot and sultry – just the right time for a siesta in fact. A *charpoy*, a stringed cot, was accordingly placed in the inviting shade under the mango trees for me and I enjoyed a pleasant nap, being mindful of the fact that I might get very little sleep during the night. When I woke up the sun was dipping down towards the western horizon and a light breeze was blowing. The giant trees were already casting deep and ominous looking shadows on the gravelly ground. It was time to finalise the arrangements for the night.

This orchard was fenced in on the side facing the road by a rough fence made up of loose stones, stacked up to form a low wall. This wall was not of a uniform height everywhere, in fact there were places where it was low enough to jump over, even by a man of reasonable height. I suspected that it was by jumping over these low points that the wolf was able to force entry into the orchard. Close to this fence was a stockade, made up of lengths of bamboo lashed together. Between the bamboo thorn bushes were wedged together to create an enclosure which was apparently secure from the attentions of any marauding intruder. It was in this enclosure that the goats were quartered, and it was in this enclosure that it was my intention to spend the night with the goats, with a loaded gun at my side, just in case the wolf turned up. To give myself some room to breathe and to afford some protection from being trampled underfoot by the milling goats, I had a smaller stockade constructed within this enclosure. Here, with an ample bedding of straw, I should have a not too uncomfortable bed for the night. One other alteration was also made in the enclosure, a small opening was made in the thorn fence, close to my bed, just large enough for a small animal to squeeze through, should it be interested in the inmates of the kraal. This would give me an opportunity for an easy shot, should such a chance come my way.

Achhan Mian, ever hospitable, wanted to lay out one of his special dinners, lamb curry, along with a number of assorted delicacies with which he was wont to regale honoured guests, but I argued with him that such a sumptuous dinner would leave one in no shape for an all night vigil and tea and biscuits, must for the time being suffice. I was about to partake of this frugal repast when I was told that three headmen, sarpanchas, to use the correct legal designation, wished to see me. These gentlemen who were the headmen of the neighbouring villages, were already known to me. I could also make a fair guess at the business that had brought them to see me. It would have been easy to tell them to come in the morning, but it has always been my policy never to refuse an audience to any petitioner, who wished to see me, whatever the hour of the day or night it might be. So these gentlemen were ushered in by Acchan Mian, and presented to me, with all the ceremony of an ambassador being presented to a monarch.

One of them was Badrinarain Pande, the headman of a neighbouring village. Tall corpulent and dignified, with an impressive white moustache, he was known throughout the tehsil as *panditji*. I knew what panditji's problem was, because he had come to me many times with it. Panditji's holding was adjacent to the Reserved Forest and a portion of this forest land had been cultivated by him and probably by his ancestors for a long time. Panditji felt, probably with some justification, that this land belonged to him. But legally this was forest land and the matter could only be dealt with by a duly notified Forest Settlement Officer under the Indian Forest Act. I could do nothing about it. This legal position I had explained to him many times, but Panditji was nothing if not persistent, he seemed to believe that the issue was within my power and all that was needed to secure a positive decision was sufficient persuasion.

He knew that I could not be pressurised into taking a decision, so the method he had adopted was one of entreaty and cajolery. The two other headmen he had brought with him, were doubtless to lend moral support to his suit. I knew what to expect when I saw the old gentlemen, but I could not very well deny him the opportunity to make his submission. We started with a discussion about the weather, then the talk veered around to the subject of the wolf. Panditji was of the opinion that the animal must soon fall to my bullet. The old gentleman was skilled in the art of flattery. After beating about the bush for what must have been at least quarter of an hour,

Panditji at last came to the point. This is how our dialogue then proceeded :

"Sir! I have once again come to remind you about the petition that I presented to your honour about my land. I will, not attempt to tire your honour with a full recital of the facts of my case, with which your honour is no doubt familiar, but let me only say that my cause is just, this land has been in our possession for many generations and we have a perfect right to it. I await justice from your honour."

"Panditji, I have already told you that the matter is beyond my powers, you should submit your petition to the forest department and the state government."

"*Mai baap,* you are our government, we know of no other, and I feel certain that the matter will only be resolved by your good self."

I knew it would be useless to argue the matter with the old man. So to humour him, I said, "Panditji, you will agree that we can do nothing in this matter at this moment, sitting as we are in Achhan Mian's orchard. But when you come to Sehore, I will put you in touch with the DFO, and if need be also send your case to the government with my recommendations."

This was more than he had hoped for and after thanking me profusely and singing my praises for an embarrassing minute or two, the three men turned to take their leave, but Acchan Mian would have none of it.

"Nonsense, Panditji, surely you are not going to leave before partaking of my hospitality. I know I have only humble fare to offer, but you will not deny me a chance to entertain you, especially when the Collector Sahib has kindly consented to be the guest of honour."

This argument, put forward in this persuasive manner really brooked no denial and the three men, after a few protests consented. Of course Acchan Mian did not tell them, I was having only tea and biscuits, or it might have prompted some second thoughts.

Dinner was soon laid out, tea and biscuits for me but for the others, it was going to be lamb curry after all. And here a problem presented itself. The problem was that Panditji, being a Brahmin, and a pillar of his community as well, could not be expected to eat meat, but Acchan Mian had not prepared any vegetarian dishes as he normally scornfully referred to them as – *ghaas phoos* – grass and straw. But a way out of the difficulty was found in a rather ingenious manner.

Acchan Mian suggested that the dinner was a feast to propitiate the tutelary deities of the tehsil, so that the Collector Sahib could get rid of the wolves and thus save further loss of innocent lives. This being the case, Panditji would be well within his rights in transgressing the traditional taboo on meat eating.

Panditji thought over this for some time. I could see that he was sorely tempted by the lamb curry that lay before him. The others were waiting for him to decide the issue, and would follow his lead without hesitation. Then Panditji, with a smile on his face suggested that he had found a way out. He said that the meat could be eaten after making a ritual offering to Bhairav, the god of death, who liked offerings of meat and drink. This he proceeded to do, taking a little meat in a small bowl and muttering something for a while. He was doing this, he emphasised only as an act of piety to propitiate the gods and thus rid the tehsil of the terrible sucourge of the wolves. This done, and religious scruples satisfied, the three gentlemen sat down to eat a hearty meal and after partaking of the dinner, took their leave, and left me to deal with the wolf, as well as I could.

After the departure of these unexpected guests, I put on a rustic tunic and a dhoti to dress the part of a shepherd and took my place in the stockade. It was a night of brilliant stars. But the moon was late in rising and the starlight was too faint to provide sufficient illumination to shoot by. Had the wolf arrived during this period, I doubt if I would have been able to get a shot at it without using the flashlight with which I had armed myself. After a period of initial restlessness the goats had settled down for the night. The breeze was blowing from me towards the animals, so the smell wasn't so bad. It was simply a question of waiting and hoping and this I did.

Not many of us, I suspect, are called upon to take up an all night vigil. For some one who has never done it before, the mere fact of sitting up and keeping awake is in itself quite an unusual undertaking. The normal human tendency is to doze off, to give up the upright posture which seems to put such a strain on the human anatomy and to seek the horizontal position as soon as possible. But those who are called upon to do this quite often, either by nature of their calling as in the case of nurses and watchman, or as a form of self imposed penance as in my case and in the case of other shikaris find it quite a different kettle of fish. For them it is simply a question of concentrating on the job in hand. If one is waiting for an animal to arrive, it is a question of listening and keeping alert. It is also a question of keeping the mind on the task and preventing it from wandering, as it tends to do on such occasions. The silent watches of the night, when the hubbub of human activity has died down and one is alone with the immensity of the night sky above one and the benighted earth below, are a time when the mind is peculiarly susceptible to flights of fancy. At such times all of us have our ways and means of keeping the mind on an even keel. My practice is to recite poetry, to myself. Try reciting, "Paradise Lost ",line by line, without allowing any sound to escape your lips, and you will realize how hard it is. There is nothing like it, to keep sleep at bay. At other times, when one is not sleepy, the prospect of sitting up at night can be quite pleasant.

On this particular day sleep was the farthest thing from my mind. As I took up my post, I felt a pleasant sense of anticipation. I had a feeling that something was going to happen during the course of the night. It was a dark night and the sky as I have said was studded with twinkling points of light. The milky way was clearly visible overhead as a dense concourse of stars. Sirrus shown with a fiery brilliance, as did innumerable large and middling stars, twinkling brightly in all parts of the firmament. After a couple of hours a small moon appeared on the eastern horizon, shedding a pallid lustre on the scene. As the moon rose higher I was able to see a horned owl take up his station on an exposed branch. I watched this bird for a while, sitting motionless on its perch. Owls have a curious dignity, a stillness and self possession that can be unnerving. This bird as it sat, seemed to be looking straight at me with a melancholy and accusing look in its piercing eyes, as if to say, what in the name of heaven are you doing here. But I knew from experience that this far from being the case. The owl had little, if any interest in my presence, and as it sat there, apparently motionless and oblivious of all else, I knew its eyes were scanning every inch of the ground beneath, like a radar. Sure enough, a few minutes later, the bird shot down like a bolt, and when it came up again, it had, in its razor sharp claws, a small mouse. Having caught its meal, the bird flew away with the mouse and for a while there was total stillness.

This silence must have lasted for about half an hour, after which the crickets resumed their chorus. This shrill oscillating sound does not distract the senses, it simply forms the background score, like the background music of a film, which heightens the drama that takes place in the jungle. After a while a rabbit appeared on the scene, looking for fallen fruit or some other object that he appeared to find of great interest. He sat there for a while on his hind legs, holding the fruit in his front paws and examining it like a scientist looking at an interesting specimen. Then, suddenly it put the fruit down and scampered away. I knew that something had scared it off, and I had a hunch that the wolf had arrived. I lay motionless in my bed, trying to appear as if I were asleep, but scanning the scene through narrowed eyes. My shotgun, a double barrelled. 12 bore which lay by my side in the straw, was reassuringly within reach. As I lay there, I saw a wolf trying to force an entry into the stockade through the small opening that I had made there on purpose. There was no time to wait for a perfect shot. My gamble had paid off and I had to fire and take my chances, as another chance may not come my way for months. So I took aim hurriedly and fired. I had the satisfaction of seeing my shot go home. The wolf was thrown off balance by the force of the shot and to finish him off I fired the second barrel into his body. As I did so I saw a second wolf, a much bigger animal, turn and after jumping over the stone fence disappear into the night. The animal that I had shot, was a young female. I had no doubt I had killed one of the man eaters. But satisfaction over the success of a well thought out plan was mixed with regrets for not having held my fire long enough to have seen the second wolf. This wolf, which had again given us the slip, was no doubt the leader of the pack and by letting it escape I had given it the freedom to cut the threads of three more young live, before nemesis finally caught up with him.

How the first kill took place

What follows is pure conjecture or surmise, or you can call it intuition if you like, but I am willing to stake my reputation on it. I am talking about the first kill of the man eater of Ashta, an event that passed away into oblivion, without leaving behind any witness or documentary record. It is my contention that Govind, the shepherd boy, whose ruined hut was described earlier, was the first victim of the man eater of Ashta. What I offer below is a reconstruction, based on my imagination, yet I am as sure of the truth of this, as I am of anything.

It was a winter morning that promised to be fair, when Govind the shepherd boy, set out to graze his animals on the pastures to the south of his hut near the village of Amarpura. Govind was an orphan who had been brought up by his old grandmother, but a few years ago she had also died, leaving him alone with his animals. Not that Govind was particularly sorry, the old lady had become reuhmatic and was always losing her temper on the slightest pretext. Now he had not a soul in the world to call his own, and he rather enjoyed the freedom that this gave him. When other children went to school, he went to the jungle with his herd, and the days passed pleasantly in the company of the few cows and buffaloes that he owned and whom he really loved. While the animals grazed, or sat chewing the cud contentedly, Govind watched the butterflies and the dragon flies or the innumerable wild flowers that grew everywhere, daydreaming or playing his own self devised games.

He milked his cows and buffaloes himself, and sold the milk in the nearby village. The money that he got in return, he used for buying grain and other bare necessities of life for himself. He didn't really need much money, and often let the calves drink all the milk they desired, not milking the animals himself. On this particular day he had set out as usual, for the pastures that stand next to the jungle. It is true that they were quite far from his hut, but then the grazing was good there, because the other village animals were not brought to graze so far afield. It must have been close to mid day when suddenly, the sun was obscured by dark clouds and a light rain started to fall. It didn't seem to bother the animals, but Govind sought shelter under a tamarind tree that grew at the edge of the jungle. It was then that he saw them ;the wolves. Not one or two, but all four of them. He would have shouted for his herd, or run out to them, but he was mesmerised by the eyes of the wolves, glaring, baleful eyes that transfixed him. Before he could shout, the entire pack was on him, snapping and tearing and it was all over for him within a few minutes. After killing Govind, the pack carried him away into the jungle, and as there were four hungry animals, who had probably not eaten for days, nothing was left of his remains to tell the tale.

This according to me is how the first kill of the man eaters of Ashta took place. It explains why the entire pack turned man eater, rather than just a single animal. It also explains the mysterious disappearance of Govind just before the first human kill of the man eater of Ashta was reported. I have of course no circumstantial evidence or evidence of any other kind to substantiate my claim. How then did I come about this story? My answer is that I seemed to see the whole chain of events in my mind's eye as I sat up for the wolf, close to Govind's ruined hut one evening, an incident that I have already narrated. Nor was it merely an accident that I dreamed this particular dream, when I sat up close to the hut. I do believe those who die violent deaths of the kind described above, leave behind a whole corpus of powerful feelings and unsatisfied longings, that hangs over a particular spot like an emanation, and affects those who are susceptible to these things. You may reject my explanation as fanciful and far fetched, but then it would be hard to come up with a better one.

This also brings me to the larger question of why wolves turn man eaters. My theory is that do so because of the destruction of their habitat and the consequent scarcity of their natural prey. Unlike tigers and leopards, who, more often than not, turn man eaters due to injury or infirmity, wolves, if my theory is right, do so purely because as their natural habitat is destroyed they are brought more and more in contact with man, and thus lose their natural fear of him. As the scarcity of their natural prey follows in the wake of the destruction of their habitat, they turn more and more to attacking sheep, goats and other domestic animals. From this, it is but another short step to attacking man.

In India, wolves have been around from times immemorial, but now very few are left in the wild. Wolf sightings are getting increasing rare, and I should not be surprised if the animal becomes extinct in India, in a few decades. On the other hand, one hears of man eating wolves more frequently than heretofore. All this is further proof, if proof were needed, of the connection between dwindling habitat and increasing incidence of man eating wolves. If this cycle of destruction continues unabated, the day is not far off when our forests shall no longer resound with that most thrilling of jungle sounds, the eerie wailing of the wolf.

Hidden Valley

This is a story about man eating wolves and tales about other denizens of the forest should have no place in it. I can not however resist telling the reader the remarkable events that transpired in a remote corner of the jungle, which, for want of a better name I shall call – Hidden Valley. The forests of Sehore are of the dry deciduous variety, mostly consisting of teak. As teak is the most valuable timber in our jungles, most of the forests have suffered heavily from the depredations of the timber mafia, which is particularly active in the jungles around Bhopal. It is rare therefore to find, even in the more remote areas any extensive stretch of forest, which retains its pristine beauty. Most of the forest is honeycombed with cultivated patches and the ravages of the timber thief's axe are clearly visible everywhere.

What is even worse is the comparative scarcity of wild animals, caused by indiscriminate poaching. The nobility of the old Bhopal state was devoted to Shikar, and though the state has gone, the passion for shikar remains. Most of the old nobility and gentry have large holdings, quite often deep in the forest, which makes it easy for them to pursue their passion. As a result of these peculiar circumstances, the forests of Bhopal division are poor, both in flora and fauna. But scattered about this dismal scene, there are still some small patches of forest, which retain their primeval glory, scarcely touched by the hand of man. One such patch, not very far from the territory of the man eater, is the 'Hidden Valley '.The exact whereabouts of this, the most beautiful of all forested valleys, I shall not disclose, in the hope that this forest sanctuary may remain inviolate, if only for a few more years. About its ultimate fate however, I do not entertain any illusions, for the conservation of forests and animals, appears to me, in these dog days, to be a lost cause. All of which makes my story all the more relevant.

Close to Hidden Valley is a small forest Rest House. This is a charming building, situated at the head of a considerable glade. The rest house compound is really only a part of the glade, the fencing that is supposed to form its boundary has been almost overrun by the encroaching forest. The Rest House is shaded by old Jamun trees, which are tenanted by a troop of *langurs*. These langurs often come down to the rest house veranda, but they are more circumspect than the red monkeys, and the visitor who founds himself suddenly surrounded by a group of langurs, need have no fears that his breakfast tray will be shared by these uninvited guests, if he keeps a wary eye on them and keeps some weapon at hand. A small stream runs through this glade, and there is usually a carpet of emerald green grass to be seen around this stream. Many a times, while sipping my morning tea on the veranda of this rest house, have I seen a barking deer, or a *cheetal* cropping the grass. Once indeed, I was lucky enough to see a magnificent *sambhur* stag, with huge antlers, walking across the glade and turning back to survey the scene with a majestic air, before stepping over into the forest.

It was in this rest house that we gathered, Siddique, Dr Haidar and I, one winter evening, to exchange shikar yarns around a camp fire. Dr Haidar was telling us about a prodigious *mahaseer* that he had once caught in a river that flowed not far from the rest house. This fish, which he had caught with a light tackle, weighed according to Dr Haidar, a full fifty pounds and was as tall as a man, but having caught the fish Dr Haidar had let it go in a fit of compassion. To me the story seemed a bit fishy, after all how could he have weighed the fish, if he let it go, but I kept my doubts to myself. Siddique however could not restrain himself."But Dr Sahib, why did you let the fish go, if it really was such a fabulous catch.?"

"Well, sir, when I caught the fish and looked at it, I saw that there were already two or three fish hooks dangling from its jaws. These fish hooks were like battle honours, that the brave old creature had won against anglers like myself. I thought such a brave creature deserved another chance."

"Really, but I can't understand it at all, such a creature would have made an even better trophy, after all," said Siddique.

"True, sir, but then I looked at the fish's eyes, which were like old marbles, scratched and streaked, but with a spark of intelligence within them. As I looked into those ancient rheumy eyes, something seemed to speak to me from within their depths. Something which seemed to say to me that we were both, the fish and I, sailing in the same boat. That decided me, and I let the fish go."

"Tut, tut, I never thought you were such a sentimental person. For my part I think these creatures are made by God for the enjoyment of man, and we have a perfect right to take their lives, in our own interest."

I could not let this pass."But surely, judge saheb, this is a rather heartless doctrine. Animals must have feelings too and probably feel pain as much as we do. I am sure they don't really enjoy serving the interests of man, as you put it."

But Siddique was not prepared to give ground, he rejoined rather heatedly, "this seems to me a mawkish attitude. Who are we to question God's plan. It is he who has provided fish, flesh and fowl for our delectation. Let us enjoy them without these morbid compunctions."

At this point I turned to a Korku tribesman, a tribal elder

by the name of Baboo, who always accompanied me when ever I was in these parts and asked his opinion. Baboo said," Sir, I do not think we are all that different from animals. Animals also kill each other, but only to satisfy their hunger. They never kill for any other reason, and we should not either."

With these wise words we turned in for the night. It was our plan to explore the forest next day in the company of these Korku tribesmen, and our destination was the valley that I have already described as the Hidden Valley.

The Korkus are the forgotten tribals of Madhya Pradesh. The Gonds, are large landowners and dominate the political scene in their constituencies. They are men of property and substance who have taken to settled agriculture and enjoy the amenities of civilization. The Bhils who live in the western parts of the state are wilder, living as they do in a harsher environment, but they too are mostly peasants and cultivators. The less well off form the bulk of migrant labourers who are found on construction sites in most towns. The Baiga and the Korkus are the true children of the wild. But the Baiga have been given the status of a ' primitve tribe ',many books and learned monographs have been written about them, and they have thus acquired a certain glamour. The Korku have no such glamour, they live scattered about the entire middle and eastern portion of the state and are too few in numbers to have any political influence. Nor do they own any land or property. Most of them live deep in the forest, living off the land in a manner that has hardly changed over the millennia.

The average Korku is a short, wiry individual who is usually clad in a white loincloth. No other article of clothing or ornamentation will be found about his person. The women however are fond of ornaments, and even the poorest will be found to have, as adornment, at least a nose stud and a pair of anklets. The Korku has no equal when it comes to woodcraft and knowledge of jungle lore. He can track down any animal from its spoor or its foot marks. He is deadly with a bow and arrow and is also an expert at laying traps.

These Korkus are the guardians of Hidden Valley and consider it a sacred place. There is a huge banyan tree in the valley, an ancient behemoth whose overhanging roots have now covered an area almost half an acre in extent. This natural cathedral is the shrine at which the Korku worship and its trunk is covered, with heaps of curiously shaped stones brought here as devotional offerings.

It is due to the Korkus that Hidden Valley has escaped the devastation that has overtaken the forest in most of the district. They stand guard over the valley, not permitting any other tribesmen to set foot there. Their fierce reputation and their skill with the bow ensures that the poacher and the timber thief do not venture into their domain. And the Forest Department, aware that the Korku are protectors of the forest, lets them well alone. As if this were not enough to deter the prospective intruder, there is also a legend that whoever disturbs the peace of the valley comes to a sticky end. For all these reasons, and due to its inaccessibility, Hidden Valley has remained a primeval wilderness. Would that it could remain thus forever.

All three of us had different reasons for going to Hidden Valley. I was chiefly interested in meeting a hermit who dwelt there and who had a great reputation for wisdom. Siddique wanted to take a look at the grey jungle fowl which were only found in the valley. He maintained that he only wanted to look at these birds, but I had a feeling that was not altogether averse to adding a few to his bag. Dr Haidar, said that he wanted to spend some time in a real jungle, while still there was one left, so that he could tell his grand children about it.

Our Korku guides made it clear that there were certain rules to be observed in Hidden Valley. The most important rule was that no animal or bird found there was to shot at or molested in any way. No firearms or weapons of any kind were allowed to be taken in. Finally – and this was considered most important – no one was shout or raise his voice. Having agreed to observe these rules scrupulously we set off with three Korku guides. The road that we were following soon entered an open forest that gradually got thicker as we penetrated deeper into it. We were descending from a wooded plateau, and after reaching the valley floor, the road turned sharply to the left and reached the foot of a densely wooded mountain with incredibly steep sides, which appeared to be flat on the top. After skirting the base of the mountain for a while, we came to a jungle stream that went roaring over its rocky bed. This stream had thigh deep water, that was gushing over at a terrific speed. Evidently, there was a waterfall somewhere close by and that accounted for the impetuous speed of the torrent and the thunderous sound that came from somewhere nearby. At this spot the road ended and our jeep could go no further. The stream had to be crossed on foot and to aid the crossing a cable made up of creepers and lianas twisted together was stretched across the stream. Those crossing the stream, took hold of the cable in both hands and stepped across the water, hanging on to the cable for dear life to avoid being swept off their feet by the fast flowing water. This method of crossing, precarious as it seemed, was the only way of getting over to the other side. The trick, was not to let go of the cable, no matter what happened. The Korkus for additional safety tied a rope round the middle of all three of us, just as mountain climbers rope themselves to prevent falls. If one person, by chance lost his footing, the others could then pull him up. With this extra precaution we were able to cross the stream without mishap.

After crossing the stream we climbed a low hill and then came to bowl shaped valley whose far side was enclosed by towering escarpments. These hills were covered with dense forests almost to the very top, but the last portion, just below the summit was sheer rock, bare of vegetation. These perpendicular cliffs near the summit were streaked with white vulture droppings. Walking through the open park like valley we came to the base of one of these escarpments. The mountainside at this point was studded with many caves, each one of which looked like the other. Our guides led us to one such cavern, picking up a rough torch made up of some aromatic wood that burned slowly with a blue flame.

The cavern that we had entered was a large subterranean chamber, which was obviously much used as a passage. The air was free from the musty odour that is found in caves, nor did we find bat droppings and other evidence of noxious forms of life that flourish in the eternal gloom of such places. It was clear that this cavern was open at both ends, which allowed the currents of fresh air to blow through, but no such opening could I discern as we went on. After walking in the gloom for about ten minutes we came to the other end of the tunnel, or so I was told by the Korkus, though to my eyes it seemed we had reached a dead end. My guides now removed a large boulder, which concealed a small opening in the cavern wall. They crawled through this opening and beckoned us to follow. After squeezing through this small aperture which had been so cleverly concealed, we emerged on the other side, and beheld the blue sky and the green earth for the first time since entering the cavern.

We had now reached Hidden Valley through a passage which is known only to Korkus. This valley is a box canyon enclosed by precipitous mountains on all sides. The only point of egress is the spot where the *Patal Ganga* river cuts a way through the mountain side, leaving the valley by way of a narrow gorge with impossibly steep sides. The river, thus confined within the narrow passage of the gorge boils and churns and roars in its furious progress through the constricting rocks, and no one has ever been able to enter the valley through this gorge. The only other way is to climb up the vertiginous heights and drop down the equally steep far side. This passage has been attempted by a few intrepid souls, but most people prefer to look at the mountains from the safety of the ground. Apart from the protection of the Korkus, it is because of being almost impossible of access that the valley has survived.

Hidden Valley is shaped like a boat, broad in the middle, but narrow at the ends. The valley bottom is thickly forested, and so for the most part are the mountains that enclose the valley. The trees that are found here attain a height and girth that is seldom seem else where. For example the teak trees that are found here grow easily to a height of seventy to eighty feet and have massive tapering trunks that stretch up without major forks right up to the crown. There are an enormous variety of ferns and plants that are not found elsewhere, apart from the innumerable species of birds, that one does not easily find in other jungle. In particular, the valley is know for the glorious ribbon tailed paradise flycatcher, which is also the state bird of Madhya Pradesh. The valley is well watered, the Patal Ganga river, already mentioned above, flows through the middle of the valley and is joined by several tributary streams on its way. Its banks are bordered with several kinds of ferns and grasses, many of them rare, and of a luxuriance and rankness not found any where else. In spite of the density of the vegetation, there are several open glades in the valley and in these glades a variety of wild life can be seen. In one of these glades is the bunyan tree worshipped by the Korkus. And near this tree, with a small fire burning by his side we found the hermit whom I was seeking.

This hermit was reported to be a man of great age. His hair and beard, both of which were remarkably luxuriant, were indeed white, but his face was unwrinkled and his back straight and taut as a young willow tree. His face wore an expression of extraordinary mildness, the large, clear eyes shone with a benign lustre, and he seemed to be smiling to himself at some secret joke. The korkus were obviously on familiar terms with him, and they greeted him with warmly, but with great respect. The hermit, for his part seemed genuinely glad to see them, and smiled with pleasure at them. We were introduced to him by the Korkus and he bade us welcome, in a grave deep voice, that yet seemed melodious.

The hermit was not a Korku tribesman. He was in fact a Hindu, who had come to the valley a long time ago. No one knew whence he came, or when he took up his abode in the valley. Babu, the Korku elder, who must have been at least seventy, if a day, maintained that he had always seen the hermit in the valley, as far back as he could remember.

"I welcome, you," he said, "my friends, and the and the honoured guests that you have brought with you. It is but seldom that I get to meet such eminent guests. I know that my friend Babu and his men will spare no effort to make your journey pleasant. In the mean time if I can be of any service, please do not hesitate to ask. Peace be with you."

He spoke without any noticeable accent, in good clear Hindi and his speech had a courtly grace to it, remarkable for a man who undoubtedly passed most of his life communing with himself. The last sentence that he spoke, he looked straight at me, as if he had guessed that I had come to the valley with the express purpose of meeting him.

Well, Swamiji, it is true that I have some questions to ask

you if I may. But first of all tell me, don't you feel lonely in this place, with no one to talk to, no human company, no friends or companions, nothing in fact but the beasts of the jungle."

The hermit looked me for a while then said, "There can be no loneliness for a man who has found himself," then said after a pause, "we come into the world alone, and we die alone. The joys and sorrows of this world, cease to matter after a while. Nor can man really forget his essential loneliness, in a crowd of people. Loneliness is conquered only when one finds the spirit within."

"How does one find this spirit?", I asked.

"By looking within, by withdrawing the senses from the world of form and colour and turning to the real world."

"But by forsaking the world, do we not in fact try to escape from it."

"There is no need to abandon the world, one can turn inwards, even while remaining in the world."

"But, forgive me Swamiji, in that case why have you forsaken the world?"

"No one can forsake the world, my son, we are all part of the world of nature, which is different from the world of men. Everything that we do, even the thoughts that we think, affect the world, either positively or negatively. Everything is interrelated and my lonely quest, as you call it, also contributes to the sum total of good that is there in the world."

"In that case, Swamiji, what should one do to find peace?"

"One should follow one's inner nature and do that which comes naturally. Worldly success, fame, money, these are all chimeras. But when one works unselfishly, at some task or vocation that engages one's faculties, so that one forgets one self in the work, that is not a chimera. In doing such work, we find peace. My work now, is to look after this forest and to see that no injures its denizens."

I felt that I had asked enough questions for one meeting, and to subject the hermit to a longer inquisition, at our very first meeting would be a discourtesy. Besides, I could see that Siddique, who had no interest in spiritual discourse was getting impatient and this impatience was not lost on the hermit, who seemed to perceive everything. So I politely, sought his permission to see the rest of the valley and resume our discussion at a later date. The hermit gave us his blessings and wished us god speed and we set out for the head of the valley.

As we moved towards the head of the valley, the stream that we were following, became narrower and the ground rose gently. The clear water flowed over a pebbly bed, and one could see the fish swimming in small pools of water. Lush green grass and maidenhair fern grew abundantly all along the banks of this stream and one could see scores of Cheetal and Sambhur feeding in the meadows. Finally we reached the end of the valley, where the mountains came close together to form a deep gorge. At the head of this gorge, from a natural spring in the mountain side, the Patal Ganga stream issued forth and came down the sheer rock in the shape of a small water fall. The water after falling down the escarpment spread out in a gentle pool, which made a delightful place for a swim. The sides of the valley were here bare of vegetation, and dotted with large boulders, which seemed to be precariously clinging to the mountainside.

It was here that a red spur fowl, upon which we came suddenly, shot out from under our very feet and went whirring away. It was here that we first saw the grey jungle fowl, which were said to found only in this valley. This was a handsome bird with grey plumage streaked with black, in size and appearance similar to the common red jungle fowl but a little more upright in stance. Siddique when he saw these birds, sauntering amidst the rocks became quite excited. He had been trying for years to get one within the sights of his shotgun, and here were a score of these birds, promenading among the rocks, as if the place belonged to them. We had been warned by the Korkus not to molest any bird or beast but in the heat of the moment Siddique forgot this injunction. He was without his shot gun, but undeterred, he picked up a few stones and started pelting the birds with them. There was one bird, standing at the foot of one of the precariously balanced boulders, who became the target of a fusillade of well aimed missiles. The grey jungle fowl, however easily dodged these stones and took shelter behind the boulder. The stones thrown at the bird, hit the boulder instead and the sharp report of stone hitting stone, shattered the silence of the valley. I have already mentioned that we were here standing in a narrow gorge and the sides of the valley were made up of bare rock, dotted with boulders. The sound of Siddique's ill timed barrage, was magnified in this confined space and the echoes went rolling away among the rocks, gathering volume, till they became an ominous roar. At this sound, the Korkus threw themselves on the ground, and pulled us down with them, and it was well that they did so, for just then, the boulder which Siddique had stoned came hurtling down the mountain, and had we not flung ourselves down, would have crushed us to pulp.

We continued to lie on the ground, till the echoes died away and the minor avalanche started by Siddique stopped. When we picked ourselves up, the Korkus were looking at with silent reproach. We had violated one of their most sacred commandments. We had tried to take life within Hidden Valley. We had shattered its peace. Their look of mingled disgust and disbelief was enough to tell us that we had now to leave the valley without further ado. We turned back, without a word and in a single file, started our return journey.

When we reached the hermit, he was sitting in exactly the same pose, as when we had left him. There was no reproach in his face, when we looked at him, though he knew what we had done. I started composing a small speech asking his pardon, but he stopped me, just as I began.

"No, do not apologise, for what you have done. I would rather that you ponder the meaning of what has happened. All life is sacred, and when we try to take life wantonly, there is a reaction. This may not always be apparent in places that are already clouded with negative emotion. But this is a place of power, and the laws of nature operate here, with greater force. Next time you take life, try to think of this and desist."

I begged the hermit to give us his blessing before we left

him. This he did by giving us each, a handful of earth.

"This earth, that I have given you, is sacred. Think of it as your mother, worship it, be kind to it, and it will repay you for your pains."

Our journey took us after about an hour's walking to a small hill which gave a panoramic view of Hidden Valley. It was already evening and most of the valley was in shadow, but the sun was still shining on the red sandstone ramparts that protected the valley. The Patal Ganga, river could be dimly discerned as a gleaming silver ribbon and the forest was now only a green pleasance. The hermit's fire could be seen as a bright star, a symbol of the earth itself and all that we hold sacred in it, reminding me of the lines from Paradise Lost –

"... the pendent earth, in bigness as a star
Of the smallest magnitude."

The last encounter

To those of you who are curious to know how the man eater of Ashta – and by this I mean the big wolf who was obviously the leader of the pack – met his end ; I should like to narrate the final encounter that took place with this animal, on the evening of 2nd January 1986.

I have already mentioned the cart track that goes south to Amla Mazzu village after coming down from the Dodi plateau. This track was obviously much favoured by the wolf, because the pug marks of a large wolf were often seen on its dusty surface. About half a kilometre south of the spot where the Rupahera track branches off from this road, there is a low hill that stands to the north of the track. The track skirts the base of the hill, coming from the north and turning west along the periphery of the hill, before turning south again and disappearing into the distance. The hill in question has a north south axis, and its south face, below which the track passes, commands a good view of the terrain to the south and west. The south face of the hill slopes gently all the way and is covered with a sparse growth of lantana bushes. It was here that the man eater of Ashta finally met its nemesis.

I have already told the reader that the wolf was unlikely to be tempted by baits tied up for it at selected locations. It needed a more powerful inducement to tempt the wary animal, and working on this hypothesis we thought of a scheme. Our hypothesis was that the wolf, though not interested in conventional baits, would not be able to resist the temptation if offered a human bait. Our plan was to prepare a human dummy, the dummy of child, and dress it up in cast off clothes to complete the deception. The clothes would give off the human smell, so essential to tempt the wolf. This dummy we stationed on the lower slopes of the hill at a spot which was roughly equidistance from three lantana bushes, where we intended to conceal ourselves. Our party consisted, apart from myself, of Siddique, Naqvi, and Ram Singh the home guard jawan already described earlier. As Ram Singh was a talented mime, he was asked, from time to time, to render the crying of a small child, and he acquitted himself with credit on this day. It was this plan, that we now proceeded to put into effect.

All three of us were armed with twelve bore shot guns. After stationing the dummy some distance from the bushes, we hid ourselves behind the bushes, I sat in the middle bush along with Ram Singh. I also had a battery operated flash light with me, which we would need when it became dark. Siddique and Naqvi sat in the flanking bushes.

As we sat down to wait for the wolf it was still afternoon and there was some time left yet before the sun would set. Siddique, wanted to have a last smoke before taking his station, and offered me a cigarette too. Siddique was in a reflective mood,"Bhai, Collector, sahib, much as I love shikar, it is time for me to call a halt. You know the work load has been piling up and there are several judgements that I have to write. In particular there is complicated civil suit, in which will take take me quite a while to dictate the judgement. I think, this may be the last outing that I will be able to afford for quite a while. It seems the man eater of Ashta must fall to the guns of some other shikari."

Naqvi who had been looking quite glum all the while, now spoke up. "Sir, I must tell you, they are planning to post me out to a production division and this may be my last shikar, too."

Both these gentlemen, who were keen shikaris, were sorry to leave the whole matter unfinished as it were. Siddique was in the mood to reminisce. "But I must say, I have enjoyed the whole business of looking for this man eater, though the only time I really set my eyes on the wolf was when we saw it for the first time in the ravine. Well, one must accept the luck of the hunt, as they say. In legal parlance, this is one case, where the proceedings have to be adjourned indefinitely."

"No, no, judge saab, perhaps it is premature to pass judgement just yet. We still have to witness the last act. Who knows what might happen this evening."

"I agree, with you sir," said Naqvi, "I have a vague feeling that all our efforts will not go to waste."

We finished our cigarettes, and sat down to wait for the wolf. The sun was close to setting. The scene that presented itself before us was one of tranquil beauty. Before us to the south and west, stretched fields of ripening jowar, a tall abundantly growing crop, with large ears of densely packed grains, swaying gently in the light breeze. Far to the west was another low hill, like the one we sat on, and the sun was sinking slowly behind it, shedding a flood of mellow light on the landscape. As the crimson orb slowly dipped behind the hill and the fiery glow gradually faded, a hush descended on the scene. The gentle breeze that had been blowing died down, and the half light of twilight, still with a residual glow of gold about it, filled the valley basin, as clear water fills a trough. Sitting behind the lantana bushes, on our elevated seat, we had a clear view of the whole amphitheatre below us, and the interplay of light and shade that accompanied the advancing eventide. From time to time Ram Singh did his imitation of a child crying, but apart from this it was silent. But the silence and tranquillity was short lived. Suddenly, at first barely audible, but then rising in volume and pitch, an eerie, ululating wailing was heard in the distance. The wolf had arrived, and for once was broadcasting his presence to the world.

By this time it was quite dark. The moon had not risen, and the early stars were too weak to provide any illumination. The wolf called once again, this time from much closer at hand. He was obviously some where in the field of Jowar right in front of us, across the road. We held our breath in anticipation. Minutes passed, but nothing happened. The silence was palpable, you could cut it with a knife. As the waiting became intolerable, I switched on the light and shone it on the dummy. It was a reflex action, done to relieve the tension, rather than out of any hope of finding anything. But there, almost in the act of springing on the dummy was the wolf. As the bright beam of light caught it unawares, it paused and looked up at us, and in that moment two guns spoke simultaneously to my right and left. Hit by two twelve bore cartridges, one of which was loaded with a ball and the other with BB grape shot, .the wolf was thrown off its feet, and lay gasping. At this point Naqvi who was sitting to my left, ran out and fired off the other barrel of the gun into the prostrate wolf. Not content with this, he started hitting the dying animal with the butt of his shot gun and broke the wooden stock. Such was his excitement that he failed to see that the man eater of Ashta, the elusive animal that had given us the slip so many times, was finally dead.

The dead animal was an outsize wolf in prime condition. Its fur was a little darker than other wolves that had been killed, and was shot through with streaks of grey, but there was otherwise nothing wrong with it. The ball fired by Siddique had made a large wound just below the shoulder, and the grape shot had penetrated various parts of the stomach and chest. Blood was oozing out of these wounds, but apart from this the wolf seemed to be slumbering peacefully. There was nothing to indicate why the animal had turned man eater. No physical infirmity, or old wounds, but then in the case of wolves there never are.

When a carefully devised plan works out perfectly, and after innumerable failures, one's efforts are crowned with success, it is natural to feel a quiet satisfaction. As we sat down, with the wolf lying between us and the bright stars of the night as silent witness, we felt at last at peace with ourselves and the world. Because we knew that the last of the man eaters was now dead and the people of Ashta could once again lead normal lives, free from the paralysing pall of fear. And from that day to this, the peace of that region has not been molested by any manner of animal, man eater or otherwise.